One Night

One Night

Melanie Florence

James Lorimer & Company Ltd., Publishers
Toronto

James Lorimer & Company Ltd., Publishers acknowledges the support of the Ontario Arts Council. We acknowledge the support of the Canada Council for the Arts which last year invested $24.3 million in writing and publishing throughout Canada. We acknowledge the Government of Ontario through the Ontario Media Development Corporation's Ontario Book Initiative.

ONTARIO ARTS COUNCIL
CONSEIL DES ARTS DE L'ONTARIO

The Canada Council | Le Conseil des Arts
for the Arts | du Canada

Canadä

Cover image: iStock
Cover design: Meredith Bangay

Library and Archives Canada Cataloguing in Publication available

James Lorimer & Company Ltd., Publishers
317 Adelaide Street West, Suite 1002
Toronto, ON, Canada
M5V 1P9
www.lorimer.ca

Distributed in the United States by:
Lerner Publishing Group
1251 Washington Ave N
Minneapolis, MN, USA
55401

Printed and bound in Canada.
Manufactured by Friesens Corporation in Altona, Manitoba, Canada in January 2016.
Job #220059

For my three favourite people . . .
Josh, Taylor, and Chris

Prologue

She feels sick as the room spins around her and tries desperately to keep her eyes open. Panting. Harsh breathing sounds fill her ears and she pushes against the weight on her chest. The room spins again, then goes dark. Merciful blackness that pulls her under until she feels nothing.

She wakes up alone in the dark room, her head pounding, her mouth like cotton. She struggles to sit up. Her muscles ache and she feels a sharp pain between her legs. She has no idea how long she's been in this room that smells sour and slightly sweet . . . like sweat and something she doesn't dare think about. Her head feels like it's going to split in half as she pulls down her top that has been pushed up under her arms. She smooths her skirt back over her thighs and a tear slides down her cheek. She wipes it away angrily before gathering her hair in a messy ponytail and staggering into the brightly lit, catastrophically noisy hallway. She glances up and meets the eyes of a classmate, who whispers to her friend as she passes. She hears two words and her face burns with shame. Indian slut.

Chapter 1

Sisters

Luna Begay sat hunched over her desk, surrounded by piles of books, university brochures, and assorted notebooks and pens. Her desk was as ordered and precise as the rest of her side of the room, which was in stark contrast with her sister's side. She glanced up from her book, her eyes resting on Issy's unmade bed and taking in the chaos. Issy had coloured scarves draped over her lamp, clothes tossed haphazardly over her chair and bed, and her desk was covered with fashion magazines, a sketchbook, coloured pencils and, for some odd reason, one shoe. It was the biggest bedroom so they had a massive closet, which her parents agreed Issy needed for all of her clothes. But with only two bedrooms in their little house, it was a sacrifice their parents gladly made.

Issy was only one year younger than seventeen-year-old Luna, but the girls were as close as twins. They had been each other's best friend for as long as they could remember and were currently refusing to face the fact that they would be separated next year when Luna went away to university. If things kept going as well as they always had, Luna would have her pick of schools. She was at the top of her class and had never seen a B on her report card. She looked away from the biology textbook she was studying and glanced idly at the brochures. U of T and McGill were at the top of her list . . . both had excellent literature programs but

Issy was pushing her toward U of T so they could stay in the same city when she got into Ryerson's fashion design school the following year.

"How's the studying going?" Issy blew into the room like a hurricane. She dove onto Luna's bed and wrapped her arms around her pillow. "What the hell are you listening to? It sounds like a bag of cats."

"Don't mess up my bed. It's a drum circle. And what exactly does a bag of cats sound like?"

Issy propped herself up on one elbow.

"Exactly like this. Why are you listening to a drum circle?"

"Because I have an interest in our culture, unlike you."

"I have an interest! I'm just not up to dancing on the powwow trail, *unlike you*. What are you studying?"

Issy flipped idly through the latest issue of *Vogue*. Luna looked over at her, blowing a strand of jet-black hair out of her eyes.

"I'm doing a research paper on the rise of diabetes in Aboriginal people."

"Diabetes? Why diabetes?"

"Because it's a serious issue for our people, Is."

"Are you serious? Hey! Can I have your notes next year?"

Luna laughed. "Sure."

Issy jumped back up.

"If you're almost done, I could use your help with dinner. Mom and Dad will be home soon and I have no idea what to do with the hamburger we took out this morning. And . . . I hate to bring this up . . . but *it's your night to make dinner!*"

"I know, I know. I'm sorry, Is. But I have a big Bio test tomorrow."

Issy rolled her eyes at her and pushed herself off the bed.

"I saw that. I'll help. Just give me one more minute."

"That's what you said an hour ago. We have half an hour until Mom and Dad expect dinner. Can you please come and help me?" Issy stood over her, hands on her hips.

Luna sighed. "Fine. I'll come."

She closed her textbook and stood up.

"See? I'm coming." She followed Issy out of the bedroom and into the kitchen.

"So what should we make?" Luna opened the refrigerator and surveyed its contents, then opened the freezer.

Issy looked over to the a package of hamburger meat on the counter.

"Tacos?"

"Nah. We already had tacos this week."

Luna opened the package of ground beef and tipped it into a pan and started frying it.

"Okay," Issy smirked. "Indian tacos . . . because you're so into our culture and all."

Luna threw a dishtowel at her, which Issy caught with one hand.

"So what are we making?"

"I'm going to make a hamburger stew," Luna answered. When she saw Issy wrinkle her nose, she added, "It'll be good! Grab the frozen veggies and some broth. I'm going to mix up some dumplings."

The girls were cleaning up when the front door opened and their parents walked in. They both looked exhausted. Their father had been working since early that morning at the convenience store he owned with his brother, and his face was shadowed by a day's worth of scruff. Their mother had worked the morning shift at the hospital cafeteria and then went to school. The armload of nursing books was perilously close to falling as she smiled at the girls. Just as they tipped over, Luna swooped in and grabbed them.

"Thanks, honey. Is dinner ready?"

Luna deposited the books on an end table.

"Yeah. Go get washed up and Issy and I will have it ready for you."

"Thank you. We're starving!"

Her father leaned down and kissed Luna on the cheek.

"How was your day, girls?" he asked.

Issy walked in, putting a basket of bread on the table.

"Good!" she said, hugging him. "I auditioned for the school play and I completely crushed it." She twirled away, back into the kitchen.

Luna smiled. "*Les Miserables* is amazing! Victor Hugo had a real understanding of issues like injustice and prejudice. And the play has some really good roles for Issy. My day was good, too. Got my English paper back. Ninety-eight per cent."

"That's amazing, Luna! We're so proud of you."

"Thanks. Go get washed up, then come in for dinner."

She went back and ladled out the stew into crockery bowls, topping each with a steaming hot dumpling.

Issy walked past her, carrying a tossed salad.

"Can you grab the dressing, Luna?" she called over her shoulder.

"Sure." Luna reached into the fridge and grabbed two bottles of salad dressing and the Frank's RedHot sauce for the stew. Her parents were already sitting down at the table when she walked in. Issy was entertaining them with stories about the auditions.

"So he's up there, singing his little heart out, right?" She looked around to make sure everyone was riveted to her story. "And he drops to his knees and he throws his arms in the air and starts doing jazz hands. I swear to God, actual jazz hands."

Her parents laughed.

"Who was this?" Luna asked.

"Gordie."

"He tried out for the play?"

"I know, right? It was hilarious. He should stick to the chess club."

"So how was your day, Dad?" Luna forked in another mouthful of dumpling.

"Same as always." He shrugged. "The store's really busy and we're trying to figure out a new schedule. I'd prefer to work more day shifts. Those night shifts kill me."

Their mother nodded. "I know what you mean. You do a night shift and it's hard to catch back up during the day."

Issy reached for the salad dressing.

"How was school, Mom?"

"Good! It's a good class. I'm really enjoying this one."

"What are you taking this term?" Luna asked.

"Human Sexuality."

The girls looked at each other, then at their father as he choked on his water.

"Are you okay, Dad?" Issy asked, grinning.

"Yeah. I'm good. So tell us about your day, Luna," he asked, begging her to change the subject with his eyes.

Luna winked at Issy.

"Other than getting my paper back, it was pretty uneventful. So, Mom, tell us more about your class."

Their father took a last spoonful of his dinner and stood up.

"I'll clear the table!" he announced, grabbing Luna's bowl and rushing from the room.

The women laughed.

"You girls are so mean."

"You started it!" Issy giggled. "And now he's cleaning up."

Luna stood up and took the other plates.

"I'll help him," she said, then laughed. "That *was* pretty awesome though."

She smiled and left the room, the sound of their laughter following her the whole way.

Chapter 2

The Queen Bean

It sounded like every phone in the school was pinging as texts flew fast and furious around her. Luna turned sideways to get past a clump of giggling girls who were draped in front of her locker, narrowly avoiding tipping an armload of books onto the scarlet-painted toes of the Queen Bee, Ashleigh Bean. Or the Queen Bean as she was known.

"Sorry," Luna muttered. "Excuse me." She may as well be invisible for all the notice they took of her. "*Excuse me!*"

Ashleigh's eyes fluttered over her, then rolled toward her friends.

"Oh, I'm sorry, Pocahontas. Are we in your way?" Her friends giggled as Luna's hand flew to her braids. "Just go ahead." She pushed away from the lockers. "I'm sure you've got a powwow to get to or something."

Luna's face burned as she spun the dial on her combination lock, trying to ignore the girls' laughter and failing miserably.

"So what are you going to wear tonight, Ash?" simpered one of the Queen Bean's minions.

"I don't know." Ashleigh did one of her patented blond hair flips. "I got the cutest dress at Yorkdale. It's short. It's tight. Shows off all the right things," she laughed, shimmying her hips at her friends.

Luna rolled her eyes.

"That black one from Aritzia?" asked one of the blond minions.

"Yeah . . . why?" Ashleigh's cornflower-blue eyes narrowed at her friend.

Uh-oh. Luna was openly staring now, watching the drama unfold as Issy walked up.

"What's going on?" Issy asked, checking her hair out in Luna's locker mirror.

"Shhh!" Luna nodded toward the girls.

"Oh my god! Is it the latest episode of *The Days of Our Queen Bean's Life*?"

Luna laughed and nudged Issy with her shoulder, putting her finger to her lips. The Queen Bean was glaring at one of her acolytes. All blond. All wearing variations of the same outfit.

"I bought it in red. I'm wearing it to the party tonight, too. We can be twins!" The girl, Tiffanni, smiled defiantly at Ashleigh.

Issy and Luna gasped.

"She did *not*!" Issy hissed to Luna.

"Doesn't she know that *no one* is allowed to look as good as the Queen Bean?" Luna shot back.

"You are *not* wearing that dress tonight, Tiffanni. I bought mine specifically for this party. Everyone knows that. I *told* you that. You'll just have to wear something else."

Luna and Issy were openly gawking at them now. Along with everyone within five hundred feet. They had drawn a bit of a crowd.

"I told you I was buying it, Ash. I showed you a picture! You bought yours after I got mine."

Whoa. One of the minions was standing up to Ashleigh Bean! Well . . . pleading with her, anyway. But standing up to her just the same. Was the world coming to an end? Luna and Issy stared at each other, mouths hanging open with twin expressions of disbelief.

"Tiffanni, I am wearing my new dress tonight." Ashleigh strode toward the other girl and stood barely an inch from her. "You can wear yours if you want to. I can't stop you. But no one will speak to you if you do. We will shut you out. Understand?"

"I wish I had some popcorn," Issy whispered, clutching Luna's arm. "This is better than a movie."

Luna nodded.

"So much better. Not so much for poor Tiffanni though. Apparently she doesn't remember what happened last year when Brie stood up to the Queen Bean."

Luna tipped her head toward where Brie was standing with a group of her theatre friends. Friends she had made after Ashleigh shut her out of the group completely.

Tiffanni was staring at Ashleigh. It actually looked for a moment like she was going to argue with the Queen Bean. The entire hallway was hushed, holding their breath, and waiting to see the inevitable girl fight. But Tiffanni clearly saw reason and took a step back, away from Ashleigh.

"Okay, Ash. I can wear my gold sweater. No biggie." She smiled, glancing around and suddenly realizing that they had an audience.

"Seriously?" she shrieked. "Mind your own business!"

Issy shook her head at Luna, turning her back on the girls.

"So have you heard about the UCC party?" she asked Luna.

"Are you kidding?" Luna laughed, gesturing toward the argument that had thankfully passed. "What do you think that was all about?"

"We should go!" Issy fidgeted with her hair, twisting it around and around her fingers.

"No, we shouldn't. I have an English paper due. And that's not my crowd. Upper Canada College isn't *your* crowd either, Is."

"Well, maybe this is the perfect opportunity to make it our crowd."

"You really want to be part of that?" Luna pointed to where Ashleigh and Tiffanni had argued. "You want to be like them? A carbon copy of Ashleigh Bean? Hang with the rich, private school boys?"

"No! Of course not! But aren't you even curious? Don't you want to see what a UCC party is like just once in your life? Come on. Maybe you'll meet some random private school guy and talk literature or something."

"I'm sorry but I don't see the fascination here. Go if you want, but I'm happy to just go home, watch *Game of Thrones*, and study." Luna closed her locker with finality.

"I can't go by myself, Lun! I need you. Come on. I'll be your best friend. I'll love you forever!"

"You're already my best friend." Luna was smiling. It was hard not to get caught up in Issy's enthusiasm. But the party that everyone was talking about wasn't at all appealing to her. Not even a little.

Issy grabbed her hand.

"Come on, Luna. Please? I'll do your laundry for a month!"

Luna sighed. "And clean the bedroom?" she asked.

"Yes! I swear!"

"For a month?"

"Yes!" Issy grabbed for her other hand. "You can wear my clothes, too."

Luna looked down at her usual, unexciting outfit of jeans and a T-shirt and took a deep breath.

"Will you do my makeup, Is?"

Issy dropped Luna's hands and threw her arms around her with a little shriek. She gave her a loud kiss on the cheek.

"And your hair, too. Thanks, Lun. You won't regret this. Promise."

Luna tried to extricate herself.

"Alright, alright. I already regret it. But just don't leave me alone tonight, okay?"

"I won't. I swear." Luna threw her backpack over her shoulder and Issy followed suit.

"Come on. We have to get home and clean up a bit before the big party."

Issy was smiling and bouncing beside her.

"I'll do it! You work on your paper and I'll clean."

Luna grinned at her.

"You're on."

Chapter 3

Getting Ready

That night, Issy was bouncing off the walls, waiting for their parents to leave so they could get ready. She threw a pillow at Luna, who was concentrating on the TV.

"Stop it. I'm trying to watch this," Luna snapped.

Luna threw the pillow back, hitting Issy in the side of the head.

"Hey! So what are you watching?" Issy asked, falling onto the couch beside her sister.

"It's a documentary about sexual assault on university campuses."

"Jeez, Luna. Would it kill you to watch a comedy once in a while? God, you're always so serious."

"Shhh! Ms. Adams mentioned it in Health class. I wanted to check it out. It's interesting."

"Well, of course it's for school. Big shock." Issy rolled over onto Luna. "Okay. Fill me in."

Luna sighed and hit pause. "Fine. So, basically, it talks about how colleges in the United States are covering up sexual assaults on campus and protecting the rapists and not the victims."

"Oh my god . . . that's awful!"

"Yeah. I know. They're talking about how women don't report sexual assaults."

"What? Why? If that happened to me, I'd report it."

"I don't know why, Is. About eighty per cent of victims don't. And the girls they interviewed were told that they asked for it and that it's their own fault. And if it goes to court, they're made to look like sluts who deserved it."

"That's disgusting. Turn it back on. I want to see this."

Luna laughed, hitting play.

Their parents walked into the room, heading toward the front door. "Okay, girls . . . we're leaving. Make sure you get your homework done, Isabelle."

"I will." Issy leaned cheek-up for a kiss from her dad. "Why don't you ever say that to Luna?"

"Because Luna had her homework for high school done four years ago." Their mother laughed and kissed the top of Luna's head. "Be good, you guys."

"Okay . . . have a good night, Mom. Bye, Dad."

Issy turned to look at Luna, a huge smile lighting up her face. She grabbed the Apple TV remote. "Time to get READY!" she yelled out.

She started dancing around the living

room, singing along to the music. She grabbed Luna's hand and pulled her up with her. Her enthusiasm was contagious and Luna found herself dancing around her sister, hands in the air, shaking her hips, and singing along at the top of her lungs. At the end of the song, the girls fell onto the couch, giggling and out of breath.

"We really should get ready," Issy gasped.

Luna nodded. "Who do you think is going to be there?" she asked her sister, as Issy started applying makeup.

"Don't open your eyes! I don't know. Everybody. Everyone's been talking about it. Look up. I'm going to do a smoky eye."

Luna looked up while Issy outlined her eyes.

"Obviously Ashleigh Bean and her friends will be there. All the Neanderthals who hang out with them. Basically everyone."

"Anyone we'll actually know?" Luna asked, blinking as Issy applied a layer of mascara to her eyelashes.

Issy paused. "Maybe my friends will be there. Probably not yours. But you'll know people. And I'll be there. You'll be hanging out with me."

"And maybe your friends," Luna pointed out.

"Well, yeah. But you know them. It's going to be fun, Luna." She finished swirling a powder brush over her face and stepped back. "I'm a genius. Take a look."

Luna turned toward the mirror and stared.

"Wow! I look completely different!"

Issy stood behind Luna, looking over her shoulder at her reflection with a smile. Luna's hair hung around her shoulders in loose waves and her eyes with their smoky makeup looked exotic.

"You look gorgeous! You should do a smoky eye all the time, Lun. You don't even look like yourself."

Luna shoved her.

"Thanks a lot! I actually do like it, though.

Thanks, Is!" She hugged Issy and started looking through the clothes on the bed. "So what should I wear? I was thinking jeans and my black tank top?"

Issy stared at her.

"Are you kidding? With that hair and makeup? No way. You can't wear your plain, old clothes. Try this." She tossed a pleated miniskirt at her. Luna held it up against her and looked over at Issy.

"It's purple, Is."

Issy rolled her eyes.

"Yes, thank you. I know it is. You need to step out of your comfort zone, Luna. All you ever wear is black. You need to try some colour! You need to show off a little! Now try it on with . . ." She was rummaging through the pile on her desk chair. "This!" She held up a black, long-sleeved shirt with a purple design on it. She caught Luna's dubious look. "Would you trust me? You need black tights . . . those really sheer ones you have with the lines in them?

Those ones. And you can wear my black knee-high boots. They're flat so you won't have to worry about breaking an ankle in high heels. Now try it!" She turned her back on Luna and started looking for an outfit for herself.

Luna held up the skirt and top and sighed.

"Okay. But if I don't like it, I'm wearing my jeans."

"Fine," Issy called back from the depths of a pile of clothes.

Luna pulled the outfit on and faced her sister.

"So . . . is it too short?" she asked, pulling the hem down.

Issy gave her a once-over and smiled.

"No! You look hot, Luna. That outfit is perfect for you."

Luna stared at herself in the mirror, surprise crossing her face.

"I don't even look like me! You better get busy, Is. You'll have to look pretty freakin' amazing if you're going to be hanging out with the new and improved Luna all night!" She laughed as Issy smacked her back.

"Oh, don't you worry about me. Those UCC guys won't stand a chance against either of the Begay sisters when I'm done."

Luna laughed and reached up to smooth her hair back.

Chapter 4

A Different World

Forest Hill was like a world apart from the middle-class neighbourhood that Luna and Issy were used to. Music was blaring from the open window of a house surrounded by a massive iron gate. The only gates in Luna's neighbourhood were those cheap metal ones that came up to her waist and were strictly for decoration. Marble pillars flanked the front door . . . a huge oak double door that was open to a steady stream of teenagers. Luna stopped dead, grabbing Issy's arm and holding her back.

"I don't think I can do this," she looked pleadingly at her sister, wishing with all her might that she was at home with an MTV reality show on, studying. She eyed the throng of trendy-looking teens warily.

Issy looked at her sister and sighed, carefully extricating herself from the vice-like grip that Luna had her in.

"Luna, just this once, will you please relax? It's going to be fine. Can you please just get over it so we can go in and have some fun?" Issy was frustrated.

Luna could see her trying to be patient but the fact that they were having this conversation right outside what looked like the party of the year was definitely making Issy a little testy. Luna was older, but truthfully, she wasn't nearly as adventurous or brave as Issy. Maybe it was time to change that.

"Okay. You're right. I promised we'd go, so let's go." If she was being honest, she was eager to get it over with but Issy was so excited, it was hard not to get caught up in it with her.

"Yes! Come on!" Issy grabbed her hand and pulled her toward the door. The bass was loud. So loud that she felt it vibrating under her feet as they stepped through the doors and into a marble entryway. Luna looked at the huge crystal chandelier hanging over her head, mentally comparing it to the plastic lighting fixture that had probably been in their hallway since the 1940s.

There were kids everywhere and not one that she recognized. As they walked through what could only be referred to as the lobby of the house and into the party, their senses were instantly assaulted. They smelled beer, sweat, and pot, and heard hip hop, laughter, and people shouting over the music. All around them, teens were dancing, flirting, touching each other, grinding against each other, and making out. One girl took her shirt off and swung it over her head.

Luna swallowed hard, holding onto Issy's hand like a life preserver. Issy seemed to be completely oblivious to the debauchery surrounding her. She spotted a group of her friends and squealed, dropping Luna's hand and running over to them. She threw her arms around each of them, her promise to stick close to Luna apparently forgotten.

Already a fifth wheel, Luna thought. She walked over, standing on the edge of the group of girls. One finally noticed her and turned to Issy.

"You brought your sister?" She rolled her eyes as Luna's face burned.

Issy frowned.

"Yeah, of course. She's cool. Lun! It's our song!" She grabbed Luna's hand and pulled her out into the crowd of writhing teenagers. Her friends followed, shaking their hips and jumping up and down in time to the music. For the first time in ages, Luna was dancing and having fun. For once, she forgot about homework. She forgot about getting into university. She didn't care if anyone was watching. She just smiled at her sister and danced as if they were alone in their bedroom at home. They danced until she was breathless and sweaty.

Issy was still going strong, her friends surrounding her, but Luna needed to get away from the crush of people around her for a minute, find a bottle of water, and get some fresh air. She leaned toward Issy and yelled into her ear.

"I'm going to get something to drink!" she shouted.

"What?" Issy screamed back.

Luna gestured toward the back of the house.

"I'm going outside!" she shrieked.

Issy nodded and kept dancing. Luna turned, sidestepping her way across the room, treading carefully to avoid stepping on anyone. She slithered past a couple who were all but glued together, kissing, completely oblivious to the people around them, and walked into the crowded hallway. More manoeuvring.

It was smoky and loud in the hallway. An unbelievably tall guy, obviously drunk, tripped and landed heavily against her.

"Sorry," he slurred, boozy and loud, throwing an arm heavily around her. He leaned down, his hand grazing her breast.

"Hey!" she pushed at him, trying to duck under his arm.

"Oops." He burped loudly, pulling her against him. Luna struggled, her five-foot-two body doing little to move the six-foot-four drunken teen.

"Brian!" A deep voice cut through the noise in the hallway. Luna looked up, startled to see a devastatingly handsome blond guy bearing down on them. "Dude, I don't think she appreciates your attention. Why don't you go grab another drink?" He reached over and unwrapped the giant's arm from around Luna and propelled her toward the back door. He pushed Brian toward the kitchen.

"Yes! A drink!" Brian yelled and stumbled off, ostensibly to get another.

Luna paused.

"Do you really think that was a good idea?" she asked, nodding toward the retreating back of Brian the giant.

The blond guy smiled at her.

"Would you rather I left him wrapped around you?"

"No!" she shuddered. "Thanks for that." She turned toward the door, reaching for the knob. She was dying to blink the smoke out of her eyes and bring the noise level down a few decibels.

"Wait," her rescuer called out. She turned, meeting his incredibly blue eyes as he stepped toward her. "Can I join you?"

Luna felt herself blush to the roots of her hair. She wasn't used to attention from guys. Especially guys who looked like this one.

"Umm. Yeah. Sure. If you want." She stammered, her hand still hovering over the doorknob. She mentally kicked herself for being such a dork. He smiled down at her and reached past her. His hand brushed hers and she pulled it back shyly as he opened the door to the backyard.

"After you," he smiled. She smiled back, willing herself to be cool just for one night.

Chapter 5

Like a Fairy Tale

Luna followed the blond guy into a yard that was as stunning as the house. There were a few kids outside but it was much quieter here. The pool (of course they had a pool) glimmered and there were lights outlining a path from the door.

"Come on." He took her elbow gently and guided her down the stairs to the path, which led to a gazebo lit by hundreds of fairy lights behind the pool house.

"Wow." She sighed. "This place is amazing."

"Thanks."

She looked at him. *Thanks?* She blushed again, realization suddenly hitting her.

"Wait. Is this your house?"

He smiled, dimples flashing, and nodded.

"I'm Jon." He held out his hand.

She tried to think of something to say that was going to make her suddenly sound like she belonged here. She drew a blank. Taking a deep breath, she took his hand.

"I'm Luna. And yeah. Nice house."

He laughed and had the decency to look embarrassed by his obvious wealth.

"Yeah, my mom's designer did a great job. So . . . you don't go to Havergal, do you? I'd remember you."

Luna felt like she'd never stop blushing. She'd never even stepped foot into the private girls' academy that was UCC's sister school.

"No. Weston Collegiate."

He frowned slightly, as if thinking.

"I don't think I know it."

She laughed. Their neighbourhoods weren't *that* far apart but they may as well have been in different countries. She seriously doubted there were any Aboriginal girls walking the hallowed halls of Havergal.

"I'm not surprised," she said. He flashed that devastating smile at her again.

"Well, I'm glad you came." Suddenly, she was glad Issy had talked her into it.

"Me too. My parents would never let my sister and me throw a party like this." She blushed again. As if she could fit even a quarter of these people inside her house.

"Mine are pretty cool. But they're out of town . . . two-week European cruise."

"Seriously? Wow. I've never been to Europe. I've read a lot about Paris. You know . . . *The Hunchback of Notre Dame* . . . *The Phantom of the Opera* . . . *Les Miserables*." She stopped, suddenly realizing how dorky she sounded. No one her age read that stuff! And she'd never been anywhere, actually.

But he smiled at her.

"You'd love it. Paris is pretty awesome."

The conversation came easily after that. It was quiet in the gazebo. The party sounded like it was miles away. Jon wasn't what Luna had expected a UCC guy to be like. He was polite and funny and obviously smart. He was charming and attentive and he made her feel like the only person in their little world.

"Jon!" A voice called out of the darkness.

"Back here. In the gazebo."

A dark-haired boy wearing his shirt tied around his head came into view. He nodded at Luna.

"Sorry. But Mark is trying to get into the garage to get the other keg but he can't remember the security code. Can you come?"

Jon stood up.

"Yeah, sure."

Luna felt her stomach drop in disappointment. She knew the conversation was going to end eventually. But she had hoped it might end a little less abruptly than this. He looked down at her.

"I have to go in and help them. But I'd really like to keep talking to you. Can you wait around for a few minutes?" She felt herself smile so wide it almost hurt.

"Yes, of course. I mean, yeah. I'll be here."

"Great. I'll be back as soon as I can." He brushed her hair back from her face and took off toward the house. She couldn't stop smiling as she took her phone out of her pocket and texted Issy.

Hey Is. Everything ok?

She waited for a response, still smiling. Still beaming. Still feeling the touch of his fingers as he tucked a lock of her hair behind her ear. She shivered. Her phone beeped. Issy.

Yes. Where did you go?

I'm outside. Gazebo out back.

K. Give me a sec.

K.

Luna was still smiling when Issy walked up the gazebo steps.

"Wow. This place is amazing. What are you doing out here?"

Luna smiled. "I was talking to someone."

Issy opened her mouth, and then paused, realization washing over her face.

"Wait . . . a guy?! Were you out here all this time talking to a guy? Who was it? Where is he?" Issy was shrieking, looking around the gazebo as if she might find him hiding under the bench.

"Shhh!" Luna hushed her frantically in case Jon came back. "Just a guy. But he's really nice and sweet . . . and he's so cute, Issy!"

"Oh my god! So where is he?"

"He had to go inside for a minute but he's coming back." When Issy looked skeptical, Luna insisted, "he is!" "Okay, okay. But it's getting really late and we have to get up early tomorrow. We need to get going."

"No!" Luna was frantic. "I can't leave yet!"

"Luna, he might not even be coming back."

"He is! We were having such a great conversation. I know he's coming back. Look, you can go. I'll get a ride back with one of the girls from school."

Luna was reaching here. She wasn't even sure she knew anyone other than Issy's friends, and they'd likely leave at the same time as her.

"Who?" asked Issy.

"I don't know. Someone. Or I'll take a cab. I brought enough money. Come on, Is. You wanted to come to this party and I came. But I need to stay a little longer, okay?" she pleaded.

Issy opened her mouth to reply but was interrupted by a smooth voice behind her.

"Thanks for waiting, Luna. Sorry that took so long." Jon walked smoothly up the stairs, holding two glasses in his hands. "Hi, I'm Jon."

He smiled at Issy, who looked at him mutely. Her mouth was hanging open. He turned to Luna and handed her a glass as Issy pantomimed fainting behind his back. Luna grinned and took the glass from him.

"I thought you looked thirsty. You're not leaving, are you?"

"No!" Issy blurted out. "She's not. But I am. Nice meeting you. I'll see you later, Lun." She mouthed a not-so-subtle "oh my god" behind Jon's back as she left.

"Bye, Is. My sister," she explained to Jon.

"Ah. Does she have a ride home?"

He was so sweet!

"Yeah, I think her friend is driving her."

She took a sip of her drink. She never drank. She didn't like the taste of beer and didn't like the feeling of losing control that drinking too much could cause. But he had handed her a glass of white wine and she felt suddenly sophisticated, like she belonged here with him. She took another sip.

"Do you like the wine?" he asked, smiling at her.

She raised the glass to her mouth again, tasting the sweetness on her tongue as the fairy lights danced overhead.

"Yes." She met his eyes and leaned toward him, sipping as he started talking again.

Chapter 6

Prince Charming

Jon was still talking, but Luna was having trouble focusing on his words. She could see his mouth moving but his voice sounded like it was coming from somewhere far away. She felt like she was drowning. She shook her head, trying to clear out the fog that was clouding her head. She tried to get up, her wine glass slipping out of her dead fingers and shattering on the gazebo floor. She looked at the broken glass shining under the twinkle lights and bent to clean it up. She stumbled into Jon, who reached out a hand to steady her.

"Whoa. You okay? Just leave that for the maid."

She gazed dully up at him, and registered faintly that he seemed completely unconcerned, before trying once more to stand. Unsuccessfully. He eased her back onto the bench.

"I think you had a little too much to drink." He smirked at her.

She shook her head again, trying to clear it.

"I have to go home," she slurred, her hand fumbling for her phone.

He took her hands in his.

"I don't think that's such a great idea, Luna. You're drunk. Maybe we should find a quiet place for you to rest a bit. Then I can call you a cab."

"It's quiet here," she mumbled, trying to keep her eyes open.

He stood, pulling her up with him. She

leaned into him and he wrapped an arm around her to support her weight.

"I need to go," she said again. "I don't feel well."

He started walking toward the house, shushing her and dragging her along with him. It didn't feel right for some reason. *He* didn't feel right. She tried to get her footing so she could stop him from taking her inside, but she could barely feel her feet.

"Stop," she said, pushing at him.

"It's okay, Luna. We'll find a place where you can lie down. Trust me. You'll feel a lot better in a minute."

He pulled her up the back steps and into the kitchen. Her eyes wouldn't focus but she heard catcalls and wolf whistles around her. She wondered briefly if they were directed at her.

"I'm fine," she said, trying to smile.

"Whoa. Your girl have too much to drink, Jon?" she heard a voice ask.

"Nah, she's fine. She just needs to lie down for a second."

He was still dragging her through the kitchen and into the hallway. She thought she heard someone saying "Indians can't hold their booze" but she might have imagined it. Her head lolled against Jon's shoulder as he half-carried her up the stairs and into a dark hallway. It was quieter here. He walked her to the end of the hall and opened a door, pulling her inside with him.

"Here we are," he said, flicking on the dim lights.

The room was huge, with a large bed directly in the centre. He stopped beside it and lowered her roughly until she was lying down. He sat beside her and put his hand on her thigh, his thumb rubbing back and forth. She looked dumbly at his hand. She could feel the pressure but it was almost as if it was on someone else's leg. Like she was watching it moving up her leg from a distance.

"You dirty little Indian," he said, almost absentmindedly. "Why did you even come here? Your kind doesn't belong in a nice house like this."

He leaned over and kissed her, his tongue forcing itself between her lips. She turned her head away and felt the room slipping around her. She fell backward onto the bed as it all went dark.

The room was quiet except for the sound of someone breathing hard. Luna came out of the blackness slowly. Her eyes were heavy. So heavy that she couldn't open them. So she lay on the bed and listened. Breathing. And somewhere nearby there was laughter. And music. The room was cold and she could feel something bunched under her back, scraping her spine raw in places. As she swam back into consciousness, Luna felt something on top of her. It felt like a bag of sand, heavy and unmovable. She willed her eyes to open, then to focus. As soon as she was able to see, she suddenly wished that she couldn't. That she could unsee this. She wished desperately that she was dreaming.

She saw Jon on the bed with her. He was leaning over her, kissing her neck and breathing heavily, wetly, into her ear. He bit her. Hard. Hard enough to make her gasp in pain. She tried to push him away but he laughed and pinned both of her arms above her head with one strong hand.

"Shhhh," he whispered hotly against her neck. "You should be happy someone like me is paying attention to you. You're nothing but a filthy little Indian whore." He grabbed at her breast roughly, hurting her.

She felt his tongue on her throat and gagged. Felt the bile rise into her mouth, burning as she swallowed hard. He reached down, taking the hem of her shirt and pushing it up forcefully.

"Stop," she whimpered, trying to pull a hand loose, trying to shift her weight. The room spun, fading around her as he shoved his hand up her skirt viciously, hurting her. "I'll scream," she whispered.

He laughed.

"Do you really think anyone would care? Besides . . . who'd believe you didn't want it? You shouldn't have been drinking, bitch," he muttered into her ear, biting her again as she lost consciousness.

✴✴✴

Luna woke up and immediately panicked, looking around the room and lashing out her arms with a scream. It was dark and quiet in the room and she was relieved to see that she was alone. She took a deep, shaking breath. Her shirt was shoved up under her arms, and two buttons were missing. She pulled it back down before noticing that her skirt was up around her waist. She took a deep, sobbing breath as she tried to fix it with shaking hands.

Her head was still foggy, and every time she moved, she was rewarded with a shooting pain in her temple that felt like she was being hit with a bat. She felt like throwing up but she wasn't sure if it was from whatever Jon had put in her drink or because she had a terrifying suspicion about what he had done when she was passed out on his bed.

She stood up, the room tilting, then righting itself. Her legs hurt. Her wrists were bruised and she felt a sharp pain that settled into a throbbing ache as she moved. The party was still raging downstairs. She could hear laughter and music that got louder when she opened the bedroom door. She edged out and down the hallway toward the stairs, the music getting louder with each step.

She was terrified that she might run into Jon before she could make her escape but she ran into Ashleigh Bean and her clan instead. They were perched at the bottom of the stairs, Ashleigh all but draped over the banister so some random football player could see down her shirt. She started to edge past them, trying desperately to be invisible, but one of the blonds, Brittani she thought, giggled shrilly.

"Did you have fun up there?" she shriek-whispered, laughing and making sure everyone in the hall stopped to look at her.

Luna turned bright red, pushing past her. *InvisibleInvisibleInvisible*, she chanted in her head, looking directly in front of her. If she didn't make eye contact or engage them in any way, they were bound to let her by. *PleasePleasePlease. Just a few more steps. Just make it out that door and you can forget this night ever happened.*

"Indian slut," someone whispered.

Her face was on fire. *I won't cry. I won't.* She didn't stop. She didn't even pause. Just ignored the giggles and put one trembling foot in front of the other, her body crying out first from one place, then another.

She had one hand on the doorknob when

she heard the Queen Bean call out, a smile in her voice, "Jon! Where did you disappear to?"

Luna threw the door open and bolted down the stairs before she could hear his voice. A deep voice that still whispered wetly in her ear. She turned right and walked through the darkness, toward the lights of Eglinton Avenue. Toward a taxi that would take her home. Home where she could stand in a hot shower, letting the pounding stream of water wash over her body and carry away the pain and filth of that night. Where she could finally cry and try to forget.

Chapter 7

The Morning After

"Luna! Hurry up, minôs. You're going to be late for school."

Luna stared at herself in the mirror, brushing her hair back from her face, then pushing it forward until she could hide behind it like a curtain.

"Luna!" Her mother was getting impatient.

"Coming." She squared her shoulders and tucked her hair behind her ears. She turned and grabbed her backpack off of her desk. Just like any other day.

"What took you so long?" Issy already had her shoes and jacket on.

"Someone used all the hot water again." Luna looked pointedly at her sister. "I had to wait for it to heat up."

"Drama queen." Issy pulled Luna's hair, then ducked under her wild swing, laughing.

Luna scowled. "Come on, we're going to be late."

"Mom said she'd drive us. She's waiting outside. *Shotgun!*"

Luna bodychecked her out the door.

"Hey!"

Issy ducked around her and jumped into the front seat of the car before Luna had even locked the front door. She climbed into the back seat and slouched down, wishing she was still in bed. Issy and their mother kept up a steady chatter about homework, chores, and movies while Luna closed her eyes and rested her forehead against the cool glass of the window. She was just starting to doze off when they pulled up to the school.

"Everyone out," her mom called out cheerfully. Luna sat up slowly, rubbing her eyes. "Have a good day, Isabelle." She looked at Luna. "Are you okay, honey?"

Luna smiled weakly.

"Yeah. Just didn't sleep well. I'm good." She opened the door and stepped from the peace of the car and into the dramatic noise of high school. She turned. "Bye, Mom. Thanks for the lift."

Her mother blew her a kiss before driving off. Luna caught up with Issy, and together they pushed through the throng of students and headed into the school.

"What time did you get in last night?" Issy asked. "I didn't even hear you."

Luna avoided meeting her eyes. "I don't know. Not late. I ended up leaving right after you did." She felt the lie leave her mouth before she was even aware it was coming. She had never lied to her sister before and she was shocked at how easily it came to her.

"Really? What happened to Prince Charming?" Issy teased.

"I don't know. Nothing. Don't interrogate me, Is. I'm too tired."

Issy looked at her curiously but let the subject drop.

"Okay . . . so . . . did I tell you that *Gilmore Girls* is *finally* on Netflix?" Issy, who regularly worshipped at the Church of Streaming Video, was always on top of the latest releases that Luna rarely had time to watch.

"Wait. *What? Gilmore Girls?* The show that we watched every single week without missing even one episode? How many seasons?" Luna was hanging onto Issy's arm.

"Seven. Seven seasons of our counterparts, Lorelai and Rory. Seven glorious seasons of Stars Hollow!" Issy was jumping up and down, practically screaming.

"Oh, I'm so Rory. Brilliant but cute. On her way to Harvard or Yale." Luna couldn't help but catch her sister's enthusiasm.

"And I'm definitely Lorelai . . . except for the whole mom part. BFFs! And you know what this means?"

The girls looked at each other, grinning.

"*GILMORE GIRLS* MARATHON!"

In the middle of an excited jump, Issy looked over Luna's shoulder and saw the Queen Bean and her minions giggling and looking over at them. She turned to Ashleigh, glaring.

"What are you laughing at?"

Luna stopped dead and looked over, her heart pounding.

"Issy, let's go." She pulled on her sister's arm.

Issy shrugged her off.

"No, Lun. I'm tired of this shit." Issy walked over to the Queen Bean. "So? What's so funny?"

Ashleigh rolled her eyes and tossed her hair over her shoulder.

"Seems like *some girls* will do pretty much anything to get a guy who's out of their league."

The lookalikes giggled.

"Ash! You're so bad!"

Issy's eyes narrowed dangerously.

"What are you talking about?" She turned to her sister. "Luna, what is she talking about?"

"I . . . I don't . . ." Luna stuttered as her face drained of colour.

Ashleigh looked triumphant.

"Come on, Luna." Issy took her sister's arm and started to drag her away, pushing past Ashleigh roughly.

"Wow. I wonder if all Indians are such sluts?"

Issy turned, her eyes blazing, and dove at Ashleigh. Shrieking, Ashleigh threw her hands in the air and covered her face, backing into the lockers with a bang.

"Issy! No! Come on!" Luna grabbed her arm and pulled her away. "You'll get suspended."

People were pointing and whispering now. Luna's face was burning.

Issy glared at Ashleigh as Luna led her away.

"Did you see that?" Ashleigh was revelling in the attention. "They're so violent."

Her crew was fluttering around her as Luna and Issy walked away.

"Luna, what the hell was she talking about? What happened last night?"

"Nothing! I told you. I left right after you did."

Issy stopped walking and faced her sister.

"Then what was she talking about?"

"I don't know! I swear. They were drunk!"

Issy's eyes searched Luna's. She smiled finally and threw an arm around her shoulder.

"Did you see her face? I thought she was going to climb into a locker."

Luna laughed. Relief written all over her face.

Chapter 8

Just the Flu

The smell of bacon woke Luna up from a dead sleep. Her nose wrinkled in disgust. Ugh! It smelled rancid and she felt her stomach flip-flop in protest as she swung her legs over the side of the bed.

Taking a deep breath, Luna headed down the hall and into the bathroom, turning the shower on and pulling off her clothes. Stepping into the steaming water, she felt herself relax as the clean scent of the soap and shampoo overpowered the horrible food smells that were making her stomach turn. The water washed the tension in her shoulders away, circling down the drain along with the sudsy water.

She had a busy day ahead of her: two tests and it was her turn to make dinner. Luna quickly thought of, and then abandoned, the idea of ordering pizza again. She had done that the last two times and it was unlikely her father would hand over the money for a third night. She absentmindedly squirted body gel onto a sponge and lathered herself. Ow! Luna stopped suddenly, then gently touched her breast. Ouch! Damn it! Her breasts were sore and heavy, and she had a moment to consider that PMS was probably the culprit before Issy started pounding on the door.

"Hurry up, Luna! You've been in there forever."

"I'm coming! Jeez. Can I rinse off first?"

PMS forgotten, Luna stepped out of the shower and wrapped a huge towel around herself. She unlocked the door and stepped past Issy. "All yours."

She headed back to her room, choosing a T-shirt and jeans from her dresser, and quickly gathered her damp hair into a messy bun. She wondered briefly if she had gained weight — her shirts had been feeling tight around the chest lately — but the thought passed as quickly as it had occurred. She practically ran down the stairs, holding her breath as the rancid smell of bacon hit her again, and called out a goodbye over her shoulder.

"Luna! Aren't you going to eat?" Her mother stuck her head around the corner of the kitchen.

"I'm not hungry," she said. "And I wouldn't eat that bacon if I were you. It smells rotten."

Issy joined her at the door.

"What are you talking about? The bacon is fine. I ate it."

Luna shuddered. "Well, don't blame me if it gives you food poisoning."

Issy shrugged her shoulders. "Mom bought it yesterday. It's fine."

Luna opened her mouth to argue, then quickly closed it as she caught one last whiff of bacon.

"Let's go, Is," she choked out, swallowing hard.

"Are you okay?" Her sister looked at her, concern clouding her face.

"Yeah, I'm good. Come on."

Luna trudged out and took a deep breath of fresh air. Issy fell into step beside her and began a steady dialogue about her upcoming Chemistry test, the cute guy in her English class, and the casting for the school play that was supposed to be posted later. Issy was dying to play Eponine in *Les Mis*.

Luna was happy to let her sister monopolize the conversation. She was still a little shaky and was wondering if she should have stayed home. If she was being honest, she hadn't been one hundred per cent for a few days.

She nodded absentmindedly at Issy, who was still talking about the play. It was probably the flu, she decided. A particularly nasty strain had been going around the school and now that she thought about it, she was pretty sure she had fallen prey to it as well.

"I think he might like me." Issy had changed subjects, but was still talking nonstop. "But I'm not sure. I thought he did, but I probably ruined it. What do you think, Luna?"

Luna smiled at her, distracted out of her reverie.

"Well, sounds promising. Did you try talking to him?"

"Yes! Well, no. I mean, I tried. But every time I open my mouth around him, the dumbest things come out! Yesterday I asked him if he wanted to be my lab partner."

"So?"

"He's not in my Chemistry class, Luna! I don't even think he takes Chemistry!"

Luna burst into laughter.

"It's not funny! He thinks I'm an idiot."

"I'm sure he doesn't."

"He does," Issy insisted. "The day before that, I told him that I like his pants. *His pants*, Luna!"

Luna tried to stop laughing but failed miserably.

"His pants?" she asked between giggles. "What did he say?"

"What *could* he say? He turned bright red and said thank you."

"Well, he won't forget you, Is."

Issy smiled despite her obvious embarrassment.

"No. I guess he won't. So what do I do?" Luna smiled.

"I'm hardly the one to ask, Is."

"But you're my big sister! I need your advice." She hung off of Luna's arm, pleading with her.

"Okay, okay. I don't know, Issy. Just talk to

him. Ask him how his weekend was. Or what he's doing next weekend. Find out what his interests are and ask him about them. Just talk to him like a normal person. He's just a guy, Is."

"A hot guy!" Issy blurted out. "Who looks like Chris Hemsworth." She smiled at Luna.

"Okay, but still a guy."

"*Thor*, Luna! He looks like Thor!"

Luna laughed. "Okay, so he's hot. But he'd be lucky to have you."

Issy stopped walking just as they reached the school and faced her sister.

"Do you really think so?" she asked.

"Issy, you're smart and funny and nice and you look like Selena Gomez. So, yeah. I do think so."

Issy threw her arms around her.

"Thanks, Lun. Love you."

"I love you too, Is . . . but the bell is about to ring."

Issy released Luna and the two headed up the front steps just as the bell sounded.

Luna drifted to her locker in a fog. Her head felt fuzzy as she exchanged her backpack for a pile of books and walked into Biology. As usual, it was utter chaos in the class. Girls calling across the room at each other. Phones dinging with text messages. A couple of guys throwing a ball back and forth. Miss McEwan sitting at her desk, sipping coffee and pretending she couldn't hear or see them. The bell rang just as a dance-off started in the back of the class. Miss McEwan took a last, bracing swig of caffeine and stood up as everyone started to settle into their seats at various paces.

"Alright, everyone, take your seats. Settle down. Phone off, Ashleigh."

"Just a second," Ashleigh called back, typing rapidly on her screen.

Luna gawked at her, along with most of her classmates. Miss McEwan looked flabbergasted. And thoroughly pissed off.

"Ashleigh! You have five seconds to turn it off or it's mine."

Miss McEwan was one of the nicest teachers in the school but she was glaring down at the Queen Bean now.

As Luna swung her head back and forth, trying to catch every nuance between her teacher and the Queen Bean, she felt her stomach flip-flop dangerously. Whoa. She swallowed hard, fighting the wave of nausea that swept over her. It passed just as quickly as it had hit her, and she took a deep breath as Miss McEwan walked past her toward Ashleigh, who glanced up as she approached.

"I'm putting it away! See? It's off. God!"

Miss McEwan stopped short, clearly collecting herself. In that moment, Luna's mouth flooded with saliva. She swallowed, but her mouth immediately flooded again.

"Ashleigh, I'll take your phone now." Miss McEwan held out her hand.

"What? No way! You told me to turn it

off and I did! See? It's off!" Ashleigh held the phone up, then stood and showed everyone else in the class.

Luna's body was suddenly drenched in an icy sweat. She raised her hand, shakily.

"Ashleigh, you can hand me your phone or you can go to the office."

"Miss McEwan . . . " Luna whispered. She was being hit by wave after wave of nausea now.

"This is completely unfair!" Ashleigh whined. "You all heard her," she implored the class. "I did what she said. She's bullying me!"

Her minions were nodding in agreement.

"Miss McEwan . . ." Luna rose to her feet weakly.

Thomas, the boy who sat behind her, noticed and looked away from the battle royale for a moment.

"Ummm . . . Miss McEwan? I think Luna is sick or something," he said, edging his chair away from her.

Miss McEwan raised her finger into the air without looking at them.

"That's enough. Ashleigh, let's go. To the office right now, please."

Luna slapped a hand over her mouth and ran from the room.

"Luna?"

She heard the teacher call her name behind her as she ran down the hall, gagging. *Please, please, please*, she begged internally. She hit the bathroom door with her shoulder and barely made it into a stall before she heaved. And heaved again. She had a brief moment to think *stupid flu* before she threw up once more. She sank to the floor, wiping her mouth with a handful of toilet paper, her eyes watering. She breathed deeply and staggered weakly to the sink to rinse her mouth and splash cold water on her face. She looked up, her ghostly white reflection staring back. She felt better now. Maybe it wasn't the flu after all, she thought. Felt more like food poisoning, really. She sipped another handful of water, feeling better by the second. *Must have been that chicken last night*, she thought as she headed back to class.

Ashleigh was gone when she returned to class and Miss McEwan was talking about their upcoming test.

"Okay, Luna?" she asked.

"Yeah. I'm fine." Luna sank into her seat.

Thomas tapped her on the shoulder and held out a piece of gum.

"Thanks," she whispered. She unwrapped it, popped it into her mouth, and opened her textbook.

Chapter 9

Not the Flu

Luna bolted out the door when the bell rang after class. She kept her head low, ignoring the chatter of her classmates around her, and trudged down the hall toward her locker. Issy was leaning against it, fiddling absentmindedly with the lock. She dropped it as Luna walked up and touched her forehead, just like their mother always did when they were sick.

"Are you okay? I heard you were sick in class?" Issy mother-henned around her, feeling her glands and trying to look into her eyes.

Luna waved her away.

"I'm fine. Probably something I ate."

Issy looked skeptical.

"I eat the same things as you. I'm fine."

Luna shrugged.

"Then it's that stomach thing that's been going around. I'm fine, Is."

"I don't know, Luna. Maybe you should go to the nurse. Or we can call Dr. Ramirez. You haven't been feeling well for weeks. Shouldn't the flu be gone by now?"

"It is! I mean, it's getting better. I feel a lot better now, I swear." Luna opened her locker and leaned in as far as she could go, trying to end the conversation.

"You nearly just threw up in class, Luna!"

Luna shushed her, looking around to see if anyone was listening.

"Shhh! Is, come on! It's embarrassing enough without the whole school hearing about it."

"You almost threw up in class," Issy continued, her voice lowered. "You feel sick almost every morning . . ." Her eyes widened as realization washed over her. "Luna . . ."

"No!" Luna shook her head, her hair whipping back and forth violently.

Issy grabbed her arm and pulled her across the hall into an empty classroom.

"Luna . . . you're sick every morning."

"I'm not!" Luna insisted, furious all of a sudden.

"Yes, you are. The smell of food makes you queasy. Your boobs are bigger, Lun."

Issy had a shocked look on her face as she put it all together. Luna shook her head as Issy took her by the shoulders, forcing her to look at her.

"You're pregnant, aren't you?"

A tear slid down Luna's cheek. She wiped it away angrily.

"I don't know."

Issy's face blanched. "When did it happen?

Wait . . . who? Who was it?"

"It doesn't matter."

"Yes, it does! I thought we told each other everything! You're my best friend, Luna. How could you not tell me you're seeing someone?"

Luna laughed bitterly.

"Because I'm not."

Issy shook her head.

"Well, obviously you are. When do you even have time? I don't get why you're still lying to me?"

"I'm not lying, Issy!"

"Then tell me!"

Luna slammed her backpack down.

"Remember that night at the party? The guy I was talking to?"

"The hot blond guy? Of course. It was him?"

"He put something in my drink, Is!"

Issy's mouth fell open.

"He drugged you?" She was outraged as Luna nodded. "So what . . . he forced you to have sex?"

"I wasn't even awake when it happened. I wasn't even sure it did. But I thought . . . I was sore . . . I guess I didn't want to believe it. But yeah. I knew he did."

Issy hugged her hard.

"He raped you, Luna. We should call the police!"

Luna pulled away hard.

"No! No one can know about this, Issy! I'm serious."

"Luna! Don't you think people are going to figure it out eventually?"

"I might not even be pregnant, Is. And if I am . . . on the off chance that I really am . . . then I don't have to be."

"You'd get an abortion?"

"I don't know, Is. Maybe. Yes. I haven't even processed this yet. For all we know, I have the flu. Or food poisoning. It could easily be food poisoning."

"Okay . . . then we need to find out for sure."

The door opened and a tiny Grade Nine boy walked in.

"Get out! We're talking in here!" snapped Issy.

Luna couldn't help but smile as he ran back out.

"So, we need to get you a pregnancy test, Lun."

Luna hugged her.

"You're right. And thanks."

"For what?"

"For not judging me? For being my sister? Just thanks."

Issy hugged her back.

"Anytime."

✳✳✳

The day passed by in a blur of classes and conversation. Issy made sure to meet Luna outside every class and walked her to her locker. She was the self-appointed buffer between Luna and everyone else in the world for the rest of the day. When the final bell rang, Issy was waiting at the door of Luna's English class.

"So don't forget . . . read the first four chapters by Monday," the teacher was calling out over the dull roar of the students as they packed up their books and raced to get out the door to start their weekend. Luna trailed behind them, knowing that she was going to get an answer soon that she wasn't entirely sure she was ready to hear.

"Everything okay, Luna?" Miss Hicks asked.

Luna looked up from her backpack.

"What? Oh . . . yeah. Thanks. I'm good."

The teacher smiled kindly at her.

"Okay, well, have a great weekend. I'm curious to hear what you think of the book."

"Yeah . . . I'm looking forward to reading it." She glanced up as Issy walked in. "Hey, Is."

"Hey. You ready?"

"Yeah. I think so. Have a good weekend," she called to her teacher.

"You too. Bye, girls."

"Bye. Okay, Luna. We've got an hour until Mom and Dad come home. We have to go to Shoppers Drug Mart. Do you need to go to your locker?"

Luna zipped up her backpack.

"No. I grabbed everything I needed before English."

"Cool. So I was thinking . . . maybe we should go to a different neighbourhood. You know . . . so no one sees us buying a test?" They were heading toward the bus stop.

"Yeah. That's actually a really good idea. Should we go over to Keele?"

"Yeah, there's a Shoppers in the plaza there." The bus pulled up just as they got to the bus stop and Issy fished for some change for both of them and dropped it into the toll box. They fell into two seats behind the driver.

"So are you okay?"

Luna looked at her, thinking for a minute.

"Yeah. Well, no. I'm scared, Is."

Her smile was shaky. Issy took her hand and Luna rested her head on her shoulder.

"I know. I am too. But I'm here, okay? No matter what."

"I know you are."

They made it to the plaza before they knew it and walked into Shoppers, quickly casing the place for familiar faces. Finding no one they knew or even vaguely recognized, the girls sidled into the family planning aisle.

"I didn't know there would be so many different kinds of tests," Issy exclaimed. "How do you know which one to get?" She picked up a First Response test, then a Clearblue test.

Luna looked over her shoulder, holding an e.p.t. test.

"I have absolutely no idea," she replied. "They all kinda look the same. Should we just get all of them?"

"Luna, they're like fifteen dollars each! Just pick one!"

Luna sighed and looked down at the tests in her hands.

"Okay. Well . . . this one has a digital readout. And it says it's the most accurate for early detection."

"Early detection," said Issy, trying to read the box over her shoulder. "What does that mean?"

"I think it means you can take it earlier than any other test."

"Like in the morning? Why is that important?" Issy asked, squinting to read the small print from an arm's length away.

"Not early in the day! Early in your cycle."

"Ooohhh! Yeah, that makes more sense. So get that one."

Luna nodded and put the other tests back on the shelf. She turned and thrust the box at Issy.

"Hey!"

"You get it, Is."

"Oh my god, Luna. I think you need to do this for yourself."

Luna nodded. She took a deep breath and headed to the cash.

"Hi there!" The cashier was smiling at Luna as she plunked the test down and reached into her backpack for her wallet.

"Hi."

"So will that be all for you today?"

"Yes, thanks." Luna pulled a twenty-dollar bill out and waited.

"Are you interested in our weekly special? We have personal packs of Kleenex brand tissues for ninety-nine cents." She was smiling broadly at the girls.

"No. Thanks. We're all set for Kleenex today. Just this." She glanced over at Issy.

"Okay then. Will you be needing a bag today?"

"Umm . . . no. I'm good. Thanks. So how much do I owe you?"

"That's sixteen dollars and twenty cents." Luna handed over her twenty and stuffed the test into her backpack.

"Thanks."

It felt like the longest bus ride home they had ever been on. Both of the girls knew that Luna would be taking the test when they got home and they were equally nervous about the results. They were holding out hope for a negative test but both were terrified that it might come back positive. They rode the bus home in silence, Luna leaning her head on Issy's shoulder, her hands wrapped around her backpack protectively. She watched the neighbourhood pass by, noticing the rundown church, the plaza mini-mart, and the ethnic food stores. It all passed by in a blur. The bus stopped at their corner and they stepped off. They walked home wordlessly and went up the stairs into the house. Thankfully, no one was home yet. Issy turned to Luna.

"Well . . . let's get it over with. Mom and

Dad will be home soon."

"Yeah . . . okay." She followed Issy upstairs to their bedroom. She took the pregnancy test out of her backpack and stood in the doorway of the bathroom they shared. "I'm scared, Is."

"I know." She hugged Luna hard. "Go ahead. I'll be right here, okay?"

Luna nodded and closed the door behind her. She came out a minute later and sat down on the bed beside Issy.

"So?" Issy asked.

"We have to wait three minutes. I left it on the counter." She grabbed Issy's hand. "You need to distract me for three minutes, Is. I'm totally freaking out."

"I know. Me too. Everything is going to be fine, Lun. No matter what, okay? We'll figure it out. I promise."

Luna tried to smile.

"Has it been three minutes yet?"

"I don't know . . . didn't you look at the clock?"

"I was too busy trying not to pee all over my hand!"

Issy tried to suppress a smile.

"It's not funny!" said Luna.

"It kinda is. Did you actually pee on your hand?"

"No!" Luna shrieked. "That's disgusting. I peed on the stick!"

Issy looked at her sister.

"It's probably been three minutes, Luna. Do you want to go check?"

"Can you look at it, Is? I can't do it."

Issy nodded.

"Okay. I'll look." She tried to stand up, but Luna was still holding tightly to her hand. "Luna, you have to let me go if you want me to check."

"I know. I'm just not sure if I'm ready to know."

Issy sat back down and hugged her.

"It's okay. Let's just find out, alright?"

"Okay. Okay, go check."

She forced herself to let go of Issy, who walked into the bathroom with her shoulders squared. Luna found herself holding her breath as Issy stood in the doorway of the bathroom, holding the test in her hand. She looked up at Luna and met her eyes.

"Well? What does it say?"

Issy's face crumpled.

"I'm so sorry, Luna."

Luna stood up and held out her hand.

"Let me see it."

Issy held the test out to her. Luna took it and looked at the word PREGNANT staring up at her.

"Oh my god. I'm pregnant, Issy."

Chapter 10

Auntie Ruby's Tea

Luna thought she'd never be able to sleep again, but the stress of the day finally caught up with her and she was out like a light as soon as her head hit the pillow. She was having a dream where she was deep in conversation with Ryan Gosling, who was explaining to her that she got what she deserved because she was "just an Indian," when the flying monkeys from *The Wizard of Oz* swooped in and grabbed her. She was just noticing they all had

Jon's face, when Issy nudged her awake.

"Luna! Wake up," she whispered in her ear.

Luna jumped, and thinking that Issy was one of the monkeys, pushed her away with a little scream.

"Stop! It's just me."

Luna rubbed her eyes.

"What? I was sleeping, Is."

"I know. But I was just thinking . . . remember when Kokum was talking about that woman on her rez who was raped?"

"Uh . . . I guess. I don't know. Why?" She closed her eyes again and tried to ignore Issy poking her.

"You remember . . . she was raped and got pregnant? And some of the older women made her a tea?"

Luna was suddenly wide awake.

"Yeah. It made her miscarry," she said, looking at Issy.

"Yes! What if we could find out what was in it?"

Luna sat up in her bed, looking intently at her sister.

"How? We could try googling it."

"Or I thought maybe we could call Auntie Ruby. She'd know."

Auntie Ruby wasn't actually their aunt. Everyone on the rez where their grandmother lived called her Auntie. She was an older lady who basically knew everyone's business before they did and knew more about plants and traditional medicine than anyone.

"You're right. She'd definitely know."

"I'll call her tomorrow morning, okay?"

Luna hugged her.

"Thanks, Is."

She was relieved. She was in a lot of trouble but Issy had come up with a solution. And no one would ever have to know she had been pregnant. She lay back down as Issy went to her own bed. She stared at the ceiling, a smile creeping across her face. For the first time since she had seen that positive pregnancy test, she felt herself hope that everything might actually work out without it ruining her entire life.

✳✳✳

"Okay . . . yeah, it's for a science paper . . . and the moss is the last thing after the mushrooms? Right. Just boil it and that's it? Okay. Thanks, Auntie. Yeah. Bye." Issy hung up and finished scribbling in her notebook.

Luna raised her eyebrows, waiting for her to speak.

"So? Can we get everything we need?"

Issy held up a finger and kept writing.

"Is!"

"Hang on . . ." She finished writing something down and turned to Luna. "Okay. I think we can get everything we need. Auntie Ruby said if we have a park nearby, we should be able to find the stuff on her list. Then we just boil it."

"And that's it?"

"Yeah, that's what she said. You drink it and within twelve hours, you'll start bleeding. Just like you're getting your period."

Luna considered this.

"Will it hurt?"

Issy smiled sympathetically at her.

"I don't think so, Lun. She said if you took it early enough, it was just like 'your monthly bleed.'"

"She actually said that? She said monthly bleed?"

"I swear she did."

"That's so embarrassing. Okay. So, the sooner the better, right?"

"Definitely. Let's go for a walk down the Humber and see if we can find everything."

Luna jumped up and grabbed her jacket, throwing Issy's at her.

"Then let's go."

It was a perfect day for a walk by the river. Luckily Issy had always been interested in plants and could identify far more of them than Luna could. She had a keen eye and managed to spot things growing among the weeds that Luna would never have seen. She scraped a handful of moss off a rock and added it to the bag she had slung across her shoulder. It was already full of bark, leaves, and twigs.

"All we need is that mushroom," Issy called out.

Luna was bent over, pushing long grass out of the way as she shuffled along.

"Is this it?" she asked, pointing to a fungus growing at the base of a large maple.

"Yes!" Issy pounced on it. "That's the last thing! Come on. Let's go make you some tea."

The smell of the tea steeping was awful. Luna walked into the kitchen, wrapping her hair in a towel and wearing her pajamas.

"Issy, that smells terrible! Are you sure it's not going to kill me?"

Issy poured it into a cup and held it out to her, rolling her eyes.

"It won't poison you. I swear. Just drink it."

Luna took the cup in both hands and tried not to inhale. She took a sip, gagging as it trickled down her throat.

"*Gah*! Issy, it's repulsive! I can't drink this!"

Issy pushed the cup back at her.

"Drink it, Luna. You have to."

Luna nodded. She held her nose and drank deeply for a second before pausing.

"All of it, Lun."

Luna nodded again and drained the cup, then set it down and looked at Issy.

"So . . . how long do you think it'll take?"

Chapter 11

The Sting of Failure

It only took three hours. But the results were not at all what Luna and Issy were expecting. Luna bolted upright in bed. "Is!" she called, then put a hand over her mouth and jumped out of bed, running toward their en suite bathroom. She barely made it. Luna dove for the toilet and threw up violently.

"Oh my god . . . are you okay, Lun?" Issy rushed in after her, pulling her hair back as she threw up again.

"What should I do? Should I get Mom?"

"No!" Luna's body spasmed as she heaved. "I think it's that tea. I'll be okay."

Issy was crying, terrified for her sister.

"I'm getting Mom," she said, getting up and backing toward the door.

"No, Issy! She can't know! I think I'm okay now. Please. Don't get Mom." She sat back, flushing the toilet and wiping her mouth with the back of her hand. She spit into the toilet and rested her back against the wall.

Issy grabbed a washcloth, soaked it under the faucet, and pressed it to Luna's forehead.

"Thank you. I'm okay." She patted Issy's hand and closed her eyes. "Can you get me a glass of water, please?"

"Sure."

Issy draped the washcloth on the back of Luna's neck and got up. She ran the water, making it cold, and brought it to Luna, who sipped at it carefully.

"I think I'm okay now. Can you help me back to bed?"

Issy helped her up and supported her as they walked through their bedroom. She lay Luna down carefully and sat on the edge of the bed. She tucked Luna in, then looked at her thoughtfully.

"Do you think this is how it starts? The miscarriage?"

Luna smiled weakly at her.

"Maybe. Would have been nice if Auntie Ruby had included projectile vomiting in her list of things to look out for. But she said it would be over within twelve hours. So I should be bleeding tomorrow morning."

Issy lay down beside her and brushed her damp hair off her face.

"Try to sleep, Luna. It'll be over soon." She started humming as she stroked Luna's hair. Luna closed her eyes and dozed off under the watchful eye of her little sister.

*** *** ***

Luna woke up late, her stomach muscles aching from being sick the night before. Issy was curled up beside her, wrapped in her comforter. Luna braced herself up on one elbow and watched her sleep. She still looked like a little girl when she was sleeping. Luna brushed the hair off her forehead. Issy's eyes opened and she screamed, pulling the covers up and nearly knocking Luna off the bed.

"Damn it, Luna! You scared the hell out of me!" She sat up and stretched, then looked closely at her sister. "Are you okay?"

"Yeah, I think so. I don't feel sick anymore at least."

"That's good. But . . . anything else?" She looked pointedly at Luna.

"Bleeding? I don't think so. And no cramps or anything. Shouldn't it have happened by now?"

Issy shrugged.

"I guess. Auntie Ruby said if it was going to work, it would work within twelve hours. And that's about now," she said, glancing over at the alarm clock on the night table. "Have you checked?"

Luna shook her head.

"Not yet."

She climbed over Issy and headed into the bathroom. She couldn't recall ever actually hoping that her period would start before. But she was hoping against hope now. "Please," she whispered, looking at her pale face in the mirror. "Please, let it work." She pulled her pajama bottoms down . . . no blood. She sat on the toilet and peed, then wiped. Nothing. Not a cramp. Not anything. She walked back out to Issy, shaking her head.

"It didn't work, Is."

"Are you sure?"

Luna sighed deeply.

"Pretty sure."

"Oh, Luna . . . I'm so sorry," she said. "I really thought it would work."

"Yeah, so did I."

"So what do we do now?"

Luna thought for a moment, picking up one of her university catalogues.

"We look into getting an abortion."

Issy looked at her, shocked.

"Luna, are you sure?"

"Well, what else am I supposed to do?" Luna was angry. "Do you think I want to be pregnant? I don't! I have plans, Issy! I want to go to university! I want to study literature and be a visiting professor at Oxford someday. And what I don't want to be right now is a mother. What I don't want is to be reminded every single day of that horrible, racist piece of trash raping me!" She threw the catalogue across the room with a scream.

"Okay! Okay. So that's what we'll do."

Issy walked over and picked up the catalogue, putting it back carefully on Luna's desk.

Luna sat in front of her laptop, typing

idly at the keyboard. Issy hovered behind her, reading over her shoulder and breathing in her ear.

"Issy! Could you stop that, please?"

"Sorry."

Issy threw herself down on Luna's bed and wrapped her arms around her pillow, propping her feet against the wall. Luna leaned forward, staring at the screen.

"Oh no. Shit!"

Issy stared at her, shocked into silence. Luna never swore.

"Damn it!"

"What? What does it say?" Issy asked, trying not to read over her shoulder.

Luna sat back, shaking her head.

"It says you can safely have an abortion within twelve weeks."

"Okay . . . so?"

"It's been fifteen."

Issy sat up.

"Oh, shit."

"Yeah."

"Are you sure, Lun?"

Luna looked at her dumbly.

"Uhh . . . yeah. Pretty sure since we know what night the party was on."

"Oh. Right. So that's it, then? Isn't there another place that will do it after twelve weeks?"

Luna shook her head.

"It's not safe after that point. So, no."

Issy got up and stood behind Luna again, resting a hand on her arm.

"What are you going to do? I guess you have to tell Mom and Dad now."

Luna thought about this . . . contemplating how to tell her parents that their straight-A, never-in-trouble, never-been-on-a-date, seventeen-year-old daughter was pregnant. She took a deep breath.

"What if we don't?"

Issy looked skeptical.

"What are you talking about? I think

they'll notice eventually, Luna."

"Yes. Eventually. But that gives me time to figure out how to tell them and what to do about it."

Issy nodded slowly.

"Okay. I guess I can understand that. But won't they be mad you kept it from them?"

"I think they'll be pretty unhappy about it either way, Is."

"Do you think you'll keep it?"

Luna looked at her thoughtfully.

"I honestly don't know. So you'll keep it a secret?"

"Of course. It's not my secret to tell."

Luna smiled at her.

"Okay. So it's our secret." She caught Issy's look. "For now."

Issy nodded.

"For now."

Chapter 12

The Secret's Out

Issy walked into their bedroom holding a sweater and tossed it onto Luna's bed.

"Here. I took it from Dad's closet. It's baggy enough to hide your stomach. We can go shopping after school to get you some more stuff."

"Thanks, Is. Maybe we can try the Salvation Army or something." She pulled on yoga pants, tugging at the waistband. "Ugh, these are digging into me."

"Here . . . let me." Issy rolled the waistband down beneath the obvious bump of Luna's belly. "Is that better?"

"Yes. Thank you." She pulled the sweater over her head. She turned to look at Issy. "So? How do I look?" She moved from side to side so Issy could see her better from every angle.

"You look good, Luna. You can't tell that you're pregnant at all."

"You sure?"

"Yes. You look great. Pull it off your shoulder a little bit and you're totally in style."

"Yeah?" Luna pulled her father's sweater off her shoulder and looked in the mirror.

"Totally! Bulky sweaters are so in right now."

Luna took one more look at herself and nodded.

"Okay. Then I guess I'm ready to go."

"Great."

Luna reached out and grabbed her sister's arm.

"Is?"

Issy stopped and looked at her, impatiently. "Yeah?"

"You're sure no one will know, right?"

Issy leaned over and hugged her.

"They won't know, Luna. I promise."

Luna nodded again.

"Okay. Let's go."

✳ ✳ ✳

Issy was right. To Luna's surprise, no one noticed that she was pregnant. No one pointed or whispered or noticed anything unusual about her. With the first trimester behind her, the morning sickness had finally stopped and Luna found herself constantly hungry. She had cravings but not for pickles or ice cream. She craved hot dogs. Just the smell of hot dogs was enough to make her mouth water. And she would happily eat them uncooked as well as boiled, fried, or barbecued.

"That can't be good for you," Issy remarked, watching her eat a cereal bowl full of cut up hot dogs.

"I don't care. They're so good!" "You do realize you hate hot dogs, right?"

"No. I *used* to hate hot dogs. Now I love them. They're my favourite food."

"I think you're flying pretty fast and loose with the term *food*, Luna." Issy ducked as a pillow came flying at her head. "Hey, I'm just saying. Can I at least make you a fruit salad to go with it? I hardly think a bowl of hot dogs constitutes a balanced breakfast."

Luna nodded.

Her stomach was growing every minute and she was fast outgrowing her father's sweaters. Issy had been taking her to second-hand stores so she could find shirts that were large enough to cover her expanding stomach without calling any attention to it. Her yoga pants and Issy's sweats were still working . . . so far.

"It's lucky your butt isn't getting any bigger," Issy remarked as Luna buttoned up a denim shirt she had picked up on a recent visit to their local Salvation Army store.

Luna scowled at her.

"Thanks a lot."

"It was a compliment!"

Luna rolled her eyes.

"Damn! It's Tuesday! I need a T-shirt for Gym." She dug through the laundry basket. "Didn't you wash my T-shirts? I need one for Gym, Is!" She was throwing the neatly folded clothes all over the bed, looking for something to wear.

"Luna, stop it! It took me ages to fold all that stuff! The T-shirts are over here. Jeez." She handed Luna one of her oversized shirts. "I hope you know you're folding all that back up!"

"Because it's not like I have enough to worry about?" Luna grumbled.

"Umm, I'm sorry. Have I not been attending to all of your needs, princess?"

"Yes. I'm sorry. I'm just exhausted. I couldn't get comfortable last night. You've been amazing, Is."

"Yes, I have!"

"You have. I'm really sorry. I shouldn't have snapped at you."

"No, you shouldn't have. I'm trying to help you, Luna."

Luna picked up one of the shirts she had tossed onto the bed and started to fold it back up.

"I know. I'm sorry. See? I'm folding!"

Issy rolled her eyes . . . but she was smiling.

"Fine." She picked up a pair of pants and folded them. "Let's just clean this up and go." She threw a sock at Luna.

✳✳✳

"Foul!" Ms. Michaels blew her whistle and caught the ball as Brittani ran for the sideline. She tossed it to her and Brittani jumped and deftly caught it. "Okay, girls! Ready?" She blew her whistle again and Brittani threw it back into play. "Good throw! Get on it, Ashleigh!" she shouted. There was a scuffle as the girls went for the ball. Luna backed up as a teammate broke away from the group and kicked the ball out of the fray. Luna intercepted it and took off down the field with it.

"Go, Luna!" her team screamed at her.

She had a clear shot on the goal and ran up the field, dribbling the ball. She saw Ashleigh coming toward her out of the corner of her eye. She pulled her leg back to kick the ball into the goal just as Ashleigh reached her and grabbed at her shirt. The momentum carried her forward as Ashleigh pulled her backward. The ball flew into the goal and her team was running down the field, screaming. She heard Ashleigh gasp as the team reached her . . . then they stopped dead one at a time, staring at her in shock. She frowned, confused, and then felt Ashleigh let go of her.

"Luna . . . " she said, reaching for her.

Luna stepped away from her.

"What?"

She looked down and immediately saw what everyone was staring at. Her bare stomach, with her belly button poking out in the middle of her bump, was completely exposed. Ashleigh had pulled her shirt up over her belly when she grabbed her. Her secret was out there for everyone to see. Luna scrambled to push it back down and cover herself but the damage was already done. Her classmates were whispering and giggling, pointing at her. All the colour drained from her face and she glanced over at Ashleigh, expecting her to laugh and point and start screeching about the dirty Indian whore. But Ashleigh was staring at her in silence, shock written all over her face. Ms. Michaels trotted up behind them.

"Okay, okay . . . girls, that's enough. Go hit the showers. Now!" She looked at Luna, her eyebrows raised. "Not you, Luna. You better come to the office with me."

Luna nodded silently. Ms. Michaels smiled sympathetically, putting a hand on her back.

"Do your parents know?"

Luna shook her head.

"We'll have to call them, Luna."

"Yeah. I know," she said, falling into step with her.

Chapter 13

Calling the Parents

Mr. Stevenson left Luna sitting outside his office while he called her parents and waited for them to arrive. Her hands were ice cold and her leg was jumping with nervousness . . . or maybe with absolute terror. She wished Issy was here. She could face them if she had her sister beside her.

Just as she was wishing Issy would appear, her sister all but ran into the office, throwing her backpack on the floor, dropping into the chair beside Luna, and leaning over to hug her tightly.

"Are you okay? Everyone is talking about it, Luna."

Luna's face was white but she squared her shoulders and looked at Issy.

"What are they saying?"

"That Ashleigh Bean lifted up your shirt in Gym class to show everyone . . ." She looked around to see if anyone was listening. "That you're pregnant," she whispered.

"I'm pretty sure everyone knows now, so you don't have to whisper. And I can't believe I'm defending her, but Ashleigh didn't know. She just grabbed my shirt during the game and it lifted up over my stomach. She didn't do it on purpose."

Issy looked at her in surprise.

"I can't believe it either. Ashleigh hates you. She must have found out somehow."

Luna shook her head.

"I don't think so, Is. She looked completely shocked."

Issy shrugged. "Whatever. I wouldn't put it past her. So they called Mom and Dad?"

"Yeah."

"Oh my god, Luna. You must be freaking out." Before Luna could respond, her parents walked in. Her mother walked directly over to them.

"Are you both okay?" Luna nodded at her, not trusting herself to speak. "Well, what's going on? They just said there was some trouble at school and we needed to come in and speak to Mr. Stevenson." Before Luna could even think of an answer, the principal walked out of his office.

"Mr. and Mrs. Begay, thank you for coming so quickly. Please come in. Luna, you too."

"Is it okay if Issy comes too?" she asked anxiously.

He nodded, holding the door for them. Their principal always strived to make his office welcoming instead of intimidating. There was a desk, but also a sofa and several chairs. Bookcases lined the walls and there were posters of funny sayings, intended to break the ice. A picture of Albert Einstein with his tongue sticking out was on one wall. Another read, "School day sponsored by Advil, Tylenol, and COFFEE! Bring on the chaos!"

Luna and Issy sat on the sofa while the adults perched on assorted chairs around the office. Mr. Stevenson cleared his throat and looked uncomfortably around the room.

"Mr. and Mrs. Begay, Luna has informed me that you're unaware of her situation," he began.

"What situation?" her mother asked, looking at Luna. "Will someone please tell me what's going on? Luna?"

"Ma'am . . . Sir . . . I'm afraid that your daughter is pregnant."

"I'm sorry . . . did you say that she's pregnant?" her mother asked.

Luna's father was shocked speechless.

"Yes, she is," said the principal.

"No. She's not," her mother insisted. "Luna, tell him you're not pregnant."

"Mom . . . " Luna began.

"Tell him!"

"Mom . . . " Luna tried again.

"Luna, just tell him the truth!" Her mother was completely panicked now.

"Mom!" Issy jumped off the sofa. "Let her talk!" Their mother's mouth snapped shut. "Luna, tell her."

Luna took a deep breath.

"Mom . . . Dad . . . I'm . . . I'm so sorry." Her eyes watered as she looked pleadingly at her parents.

"Luna, you're not," her mother said softly.

Luna nodded.

"I'm sorry. I am. I'm pregnant." Her mother's eyes filled with tears and her father took a shuddering breath and looked at the floor, taking his wife's hand.

"How, Luna? How did this happen?" her mother asked.

Luna shook her head.

"Who? Who's the father? I didn't even know you dated." Their mother was at a loss.

Luna shook her head again.

"Luna, tell them," Issy pleaded. "If you don't, I will."

Luna swallowed, wringing her hands together. They were freezing. She took a deep breath.

"I'm not dating. I've never dated anyone. Issy and I went to a party and someone put something in my drink." She paused, not looking at her parents.

"What are you saying, Luna?" her father asked. "Did someone . . ." He trailed off, rubbing his hand across his face.

She nodded. "Yeah. I wasn't entirely sure. I was unconscious. But, yeah."

"Why didn't you tell us?" her mother asked, tears running down her face. "We could have taken you to the hospital. We could have called the police!"

"I don't know," Luna admitted. "At first, I was scared. I was in shock. I wasn't even sure what happened and I didn't want to face what might have happened. So I tried to forget about it. I thought if I pretended it didn't happen, I could just let it go and move on. But then I found out that I was pregnant. And I was terrified. I tried to get rid of it. I thought I could make Auntie Ruby's miscarriage tea and that would be that. You'd never have to know. I wouldn't have to disappoint you."

Her parents exchanged glances.

"Luna, I know you must have been scared. But how could we be disappointed in you? You were raped. Who was it? Whoever it was should be held accountable."

Luna shook her head.

"No. I'm not telling you that. I know how they treat rape victims and I'm not going to have everyone staring and calling me a dirty Indian slut or telling me that I deserved it!"

Mr. Stevenson had been quiet throughout

this exchange. He looked completely shocked. He cleared his throat.

"Luna, I'm going to let you take the rest of the week off. I'll make sure you can make up any assignments you miss. But I think you need some time to just concentrate on this with your parents and try to come up with a solution." He looked at her parents. "I'm here for all of you. Anything I can do for you, please don't hesitate to ask. Luna has a place here, no matter what." He stood and held out his hand to her parents, offering a warm handshake. "Let's talk again in a couple of days."

Luna and Issy followed their parents out the door and into the hallway.

"You may as well come home too, Isabelle," their mother said.

They headed to the parking lot and climbed into the car, pulling away from the school. It was a silent ride home. Only the occasional sniffle from their mother broke the silence. When they reached the house, the girls jumped out and headed up to their room before either of their parents could stop them. Or worse, try to talk to them.

"Are you okay?" Issy asked, throwing herself down on her bed.

Luna undid the top button of her jeans, letting out a sigh of relief.

"Yeah. I'm glad it's out in the open. With Mom and Dad, I mean. It's going to be another story going back to school. Everyone knows. They'll be talking about me. They already think I'm some dirty Indian. What will they think now? That I'm a teen mother whose baby will be born with fetal alcohol syndrome?"

"Who cares? Anyone who matters at all won't be whispering. They know what kind of person you are. And anyone who talks about you isn't someone you need in your life anyway."

"I know. But it's the pointing and whispering. They'll be trying to catch a glimpse of my stomach." She grimaced.

"So let them! Let them stare! I'll be standing right beside you. And I'm never going to judge you."

"I know you won't. You're my best friend, Is." She hugged Issy hard.

"You know you're going to have to make a decision soon, right?"

"Yeah. I know."

Chapter 14

A Week Off

There was a soft knock on the door and their mother stepped in.

"Issy, can you go help your father? I'd like to speak to your sister alone, please."

Issy glanced at Luna, her eyebrows raised. She stood up and walked past her mother, pausing to kiss her on the cheek and murmur "go easy on her" before she left the room.

Luna's mother looked tired. She sat on the bed and reached over to Luna, pushing a strand of hair behind her ear. That small gesture filled her eyes with tears. She fell into her mother's arms and cried. Her mom rocked her gently, stroking her hair and hushing her.

"I'm so sorry, Mom," sobbed Luna, as if her heart was breaking.

"Oh, Luna, I'm not mad at you." Her mother pulled her up to look into her eyes, her face filled with sorrow. "I'm so sorry you had to go through that. That you were attacked by that boy." Her face turned angry. "I wish you'd tell me who it was. He shouldn't get away with it, Luna. Not with the attack and not with your pregnancy."

"I can't, Mom. If I report it, I'll have to go to court. Do you know what they do to girls like me in court?"

Her mother shrugged.

"They call them whores. They tell them that they were asking for it. That they shouldn't have dressed the way they dressed. That they deserved it. I can't."

"I'm trying to respect that. But I want you to know something. I don't blame you. You're the victim here, Luna. What happened to you wasn't your fault. You didn't deserve it. You know that, right?"

Luna nodded.

"I know. But everyone knows I'm pregnant now. They're going to be talking about me."

Her mother lifted her chin.

"Let them. But Luna . . . you shouldn't be the one responsible for his actions. Not for people talking and not for this child. Have you thought about what you want to do when the baby is born?"

Luna shook her head. "I'm not sure. I've spent so long trying to hide it that I haven't really sat down and thought about what happens next."

Her mother nodded. "Then we have to start thinking about it. Together."

"I know."

Her mom hugged her again.

"And I know you don't want to say who the father is . . . but please consider telling me. Let me help you. You wouldn't have to face him alone, Luna. Now there's four of us."

Luna rubbed her stomach. "Five," she said.

Her mother smiled sadly.

"Yes. Now we're five."

✳ ✳ ✳

The rest of the week passed in a blur. Luna spent most of it doing her homework, taking long walks along the river by herself, and reading a book that her mother had bought for her, called *What to Expect When You're Expecting.* It was fascinating. She could see what her baby looked like week-by-week and read about how it was developing. She was almost six months pregnant. Nearly into her third trimester and she had missed so much!

"Did you know the baby can grab things?" she asked Issy. Issy looked up from her book.

"Seriously? Like what?"

Luna flipped a page.

"It doesn't say. But if there was something there in front of him, he could grab it."

"He?"

Luna blushed.

"I don't like calling the baby 'it.' He feels like a boy."

"Have you felt him move?" Issy asked, reaching out to touch Luna's belly.

She shook her head.

"I don't think so. I mean, maybe. But it's more like fluttering, so I'm not really sure." She looked down at her book again. "He has tiny little fingernails now. Isn't that amazing?"

"Wait . . . he didn't always have fingernails?" Issy peered at the illustration in the book.

"Nope," Luna smiled. "He has eyelids and eyebrows now too. He's like a little person in there." She rubbed her belly, smiling softly.

Issy watched her, frowning.

"So . . . Luna . . . are you thinking of keeping him?"

Luna closed the book and sighed.

"I don't know. I didn't know I'd be so attached to him. I can't imagine giving him to someone else to raise. But I can't imagine being a mother either. I had my whole life mapped out, Is. I knew where I'd go to school, what I'd study, and where I'd work. I knew when I'd get married and have kids. And it was a long time from now." She looked pleadingly at her sister. "What do I do, Is?"

"I can't tell you what to do with your baby, Luna. But I think you should keep it. You wouldn't have to do it all alone. I could help. Mom and Dad could help too."

"But, everything would change, Is. How would we afford a baby? Who'd take care of him? Dad's store is so busy, he's almost never home. Mom works and goes to school. You have one more year and then you're going to university, too. It's not fair to ask everyone to make sacrifices for me."

"But it wouldn't just be for you."

"I know that. I do. But I have to look at what kind of life I could give him, Is." She rubbed her stomach. "But Is . . . I already love him."

"I know you do. That's why you have to figure out what's best for him."

Luna nodded and tried to imagine what her life would be like with a baby. And what it would be like without him.

Chapter 15

The Queen Bean Has a Change of Heart

On Monday morning, Luna put on yoga pants and a long-sleeved shirt and stared at herself in the bathroom mirror. She turned sideways, sucking her stomach in. It was no use. Her stomach was impossible to hide and . . . there was something else.

"Is!" she called out, turning to the other side, then side to side.

"What?"

"Come here."

Issy walked into the bathroom, applying deodorant under her arms.

"Yeah?"

"My boobs are freakin' huge! I look pregnant!" She turned sideways, the faced Issy directly.

"You *are* pregnant! And your boobs look amazing. I wish I had boobs like that." She looked at herself in the mirror, and then shrugged. "We're going to be late." She turned to leave but Luna grabbed her arm.

"They're all going to be talking about me. I can't stand the thought of walking in and having people pointing and whispering, 'Oh look . . . there's the pregnant girl! Oh my god . . . she's huge! She's such a slut!'" Luna was whispering in an exaggerated shriek that made Issy giggle despite the fact that her sister was obviously freaking out.

"So let them talk. Yeah, they'll probably talk. But so what? This week it's the fact that you're pregnant. Next week it'll be something else. That's high school."

"Yeah, well . . . it's not that easy to ignore when it's about you." Luna picked an oversized sweater off the counter and pulled it on to hide her shape and headed out of the bathroom. Issy grabbed her arm to stop her.

"I know. I'm sorry. But they don't matter, Luna."

Luna nodded and gave her a half-smile, pulling her toward the door.

"Come on. Let's just get this over with."

They walked to school with Luna pulling at her sweater constantly, trying to find the best way to make it fall so it hid as much of her as possible. Issy kept up a steady chatter of gossip she had heard from her friends just to fill the silence.

"So I heard Cameron dumped Raj and is going out with JJ now!" she said, jumping up and down in front of Luna.

Despite her grey mood, Luna found herself suddenly interested in her sister's gossip.

"Really? I thought JJ was dating whatshername. The skinny one with the weird facial piercing."

"Nicole. And no. That's his twin, Joel."

They got to school with Issy still jumping around and Luna's heart feeling like it was beating out of her chest. She followed Issy into the school and started down the hall toward her locker, keeping her head down and wishing in vain that she was invisible.

For a minute she felt like she *was* invisible. No one was talking. No one even seemed to notice her. Maybe she had been wrong. Maybe they had spent last week talking about her, and now they had moved on to Marni Thompson's nose job or the Gym teacher who was sleeping with one of the women who worked in the cafeteria. A smile teased the corners of her mouth and she got to her locker without hearing any snide comments or whispers directed at her.

Issy leaned against the lockers while Luna

spun her lock and opened the door, breathing a sigh of relief. She was about to comment about it to Issy when she saw Ashleigh Bean walking toward her with her coven gathered around her. Brittani saw Luna and turned to Ashleigh, tossing her hair over one shoulder.

"Oh my god . . . I know they have to let her back in . . . but I can't believe she had the nerve to show her face here."

Luna heard the giggles, titters, and cackles bouncing off the walls around her, which suddenly felt like they were closing in. Her face was on fire and she couldn't swallow. Issy grabbed her hand and squeezed it.

"I know, right?" another voice broke in. "And who does she think she's fooling with that giant sweater? Umm . . . hello, Teen Mom? We can see your preggo belly!"

More laughter. More people turning to look and straining to hear what was going on. Luna's free hand automatically moved protectively over her stomach.

"If she was smart, she would have stayed home instead of showing off what a filthy little Indian whore she is," Brittani cackled.

The colour drained out of Luna's face. Issy dropped her backpack, opening her mouth to confront the girls. But before she could, Ashleigh Bean stopped dead in the middle of the hall and turned on her heel. She glared at her friends, hands on her tiny hips.

"Hey! Shut your mouth, Brittani. I mean it. That goes for all of you. She belongs here just as much as any of us. Just leave her alone or you can find somewhere else to sit for lunch today."

Her friends were gobsmacked. Every one of them was shocked into silence. But no one was more shocked than Luna and Issy. They looked at each other, mouths open.

"Did she just . . . ?" Issy trailed off.

Luna nodded, too stunned to speak. Ashleigh tossed her hair and turned her back on her minions, resuming her walk down the hall to her class. She passed Luna and Issy and nodded at them slightly. Luna looked at Issy and raised her eyebrows. Issy shook her head, utterly speechless.

✳ ✳ ✳

Luna was on her fourth bathroom break of the day. She felt like she couldn't get through one class without running to pee. Her teachers were sympathetic and allowed her to leave without making a big deal out of it. She flushed and walked out of the stall, smoothing her sweater. She leaned against the sink and looked at herself in the mirror. She looked exhausted but the stress lines in her forehead had eased since that morning. As she turned on the water, the bathroom door opened to her right. She looked up and came face to face with Ashleigh Bean. She looked away quickly and turned off the faucet, shaking the water from her hands. To her surprise, Ashleigh handed her a paper towel.

"Umm . . . thanks?" She took it and dried her hands.

Ashleigh stood in front of her, not moving. She cleared her throat.

"So hey . . . listen . . . I just wanted to say that I think it's really brave of you to come back like this . . . after what happened to you . . . at the party." She cleared her throat before continuing. "You must have known people would talk. That can't be easy."

Luna felt like someone could, quite literally, knock her over with a feather.

"Yes! I mean, no. It was hard. I thought I was in the clear but then . . ."

"Yeah . . . then. They won't bother you again."

"Thanks for that. I don't know what to say . . . but thanks."

Ashleigh nodded.

Luna went to move around her to the door, but stopped and looked at her again. "But why? I thought you hated me. Why would you stick up for me?"

Ashleigh opened her mouth, then closed it. It was the first time that Luna had ever seen her look unsure of herself and she had a sudden urge to bail her out.

"Hey . . . it's okay. You don't have to answer. I just appreciate that you did that." She smiled and turned back to the door.

"I had an abortion last year!" Ashleigh blurted out.

Luna turned around and stared at her, mouth open.

"No one knows," she warned. "I didn't tell anyone."

"I swear . . . I won't say anything. You can trust me."

Ashleigh nodded, smiling slightly.

"If I had kept it, they would have been saying those things about me. So . . . I know how you must feel."

"Well . . . thanks. I appreciate it. I *do* appreciate it."

Ashleigh nodded. "And . . . if you ever need to talk about it . . . with someone who knows how you feel . . ." She scribbled on a paper towel. "You can text me. If you want to." She handed it to Luna, who took it and shoved it into her pocket.

"I . . . okay . . . thanks. I mean it. Thank you."

Ashleigh nodded and smiled. The first real, genuine smile she had ever smiled at Luna.

"You'll be okay, Luna."

Luna smiled widely back at her, then Ashleigh left the washroom. As Luna looked at herself in the mirror, she felt the baby move inside her. The first real movement she had felt. She smiled and rubbed her stomach. Suddenly, she didn't feel quite so alone in all of this.

Chapter 16

A Victim No More

Issy met Luna at the door to her last class and they fell into step, walking to Luna's locker to collect her books.

"So that was pretty crazy this morning," Issy blurted out.

Luna nodded. "I know, right?"

Issy gawked at her. "That's it? That's all you have to say?"

Luna shrugged.

"Lun, Ashleigh Bean — the Queen Bean

herself — stood up to her friends for you. This is huge!"

Luna nodded again, not meeting Issy's eyes. She was absolutely bursting to tell her about her conversation with Ashleigh but she had promised not to tell anyone. *But surely I could tell my sister*, she argued with herself. She glanced at Issy, who had gone quiet all of a sudden. She was looking suspiciously back at her.

"What are you not telling me?" she asked.

Luna looked away guiltily.

"Nothing!"

"Oh my god, Luna! You're the worst liar in the world!"

They got to Luna's locker and immediately people were staring at her. They were craning their necks to catch a glimpse of her stomach. The hall was buzzing with activity, but not enough that they didn't hear the whispers about Luna around them.

"Shut up!" Issy yelled at the two whispering girls one bank of lockers over.

Luna jumped and stared at Issy in shock.

"Is . . . " she started, as Ashleigh Bean came into view.

Ashleigh sashayed toward them, smiling at the lucky few who rated her momentary attention. Issy glared at the whispering girls until they scampered off down the hall.

"Bitches," Issy shouted after them. "I swear to God, if I hear you talking about her again, I will rip your throat out."

"Isabelle!" Luna was shocked at Issy's violent temper but was distracted by the rapid approach of the Queen Bean.

"Have a good night, Luna," said Ashleigh and waved as she swept past them.

Issy turned to stare at her sister.

"Umm . . . thanks. You too," Luna called back weakly.

Issy turned on her heel and stormed off toward the front door, leaving Luna to grab her books, slam closed her locker, and run after her.

"Issy, wait up!" She caught up to her outside.

Issy turned, her eyes full of anger.

"What the hell is going on, Luna? And tell the truth! I have stood by you and I've lied for you. I don't deserve to have you lying to me about Ashleigh Bean!" Her eyes were narrowed as she studied a panting Luna.

"Okay! But not right in front of the school. I promised not to tell anyone, Is. This is huge. I don't want anyone to hear us."

A group of girls walked past them and giggled.

"Cross my heart and hope to die. Oh, piss off!" Issy screamed.

The girls stopped laughing and ran across the street, away from Issy.

"Come on, Is. You have to stop yelling at everyone who looks at me funny."

"Yeah, well . . . we're going to talk about that, too. But you first." They were a block from the school now, and the crowd of students was thinning out. "So what's the deal with you and Ashleigh Bean all of a sudden?"

Luna looked at her and then took her arm to pull her even farther down the street.

"Ashleigh stood up for me because she knows how I feel."

Issy looked at her quizzically.

"What are you talking about? How you feel about what?"

"About being pregnant. She knows how I feel because she was pregnant last year."

Issy's mouth dropped open.

"*What?* No, she wasn't. She's messing with you, Luna. Everyone would have known."

"She was. But nobody knew because she had an abortion and didn't tell anyone. She even gave me her number in case I needed to talk."

She waved the number at Issy, who looked like she was about to pass out.

"You have *me* to talk to." She grabbed the bit of paper, fished her phone out of her bag, and dialled the number.

"What are you doing?" Luna gasped,

grabbing for her hand. Issy smacked her hand away.

"Finding out if this is actually her number. Hello? Oh, hi. Is Bob there? Oh, I'm sorry. I must have dialled wrong. Thanks." She hung up. "Well, it's definitely her number. Wow. I can't even believe this."

"Well, keep it to yourself, Is. I wasn't supposed to tell anyone."

"I will. I promise. But, wow. I can't wrap my head around it."

Luna nodded.

"I know. Crazy."

"Are you going to call her?"

"I don't know. Probably not. She's been awful to us for years. It's hard to consider having a friendly chat. Even now."

"Yeah. Listen. There's something else I wanted to talk to you about."

"Okay."

Issy took a deep breath.

"You know I love you and you know I've

been there for you this whole time. But I hate the way people are talking about you and laughing at you, and none of this is even your fault!"

Luna nodded at her.

"But none of them know that, Is."

"Then tell them!"

Luna shook her head.

"No. It's bad enough that they all know I'm pregnant. I don't want everyone to know I was raped, too."

"But it's not fair! He's getting away with raping you *and* the pregnancy? He should be laughed at and pointed at too!"

"He doesn't even know I'm pregnant, Is."

"Then tell him! He should have to help you, Luna."

Luna looked at her for a moment and then shook her head.

"I don't want to talk to him. I don't want anything to do with him."

"Then let me do it. It's not fair, Luna. He

should have to deal with the stress and the shame too. I hate that double standard."

Luna sighed deeply.

"You'd call? I wouldn't have to talk to him?"

"Nope. You can just sit there and watch me shoot that idiot down."

Luna smiled slightly.

"Okay. And you know what? You're right! He should have to deal with this, too!"

Issy fake-punched her in the shoulder.

"That's the spirit."

"But how do we get his number?"

Issy winked.

"I already checked his Facebook page. The idiot has a public profile and he posted his number on it." She pulled it up on her phone and started dialling right there.

"Wait! Issy, hang on. I'm not sure we should do this!"

Issy easily batted her away and shushed her.

"It's ringing. Hello? Is this Jon? It is? Great.

So, Jon, I've got great news for you. You're going to be a father! No. No, I'm not kidding. What do you mean, who is this? Why? How many girls have you drugged and raped recently?" Issy's voice was going up in pitch and volume. "Yeah, well, that's exactly what you did to my sister, Luna. Oh, you remember her, do you? *What*? What did you just say? You're crazy! You're the only one she's *ever* slept with and she wouldn't have even slept with you if you hadn't forced her. Yes, you did. She is not! Yeah, well . . . she doesn't want your money! And I swear to God if I hear that you do this to anyone else . . ." She looked at the phone, then at Luna. "He hung up."

"Well, what did he say?"

"Luna, he's an idiot. He's a rapist and an idiot."

Luna touched her arm.

"It's okay. You can tell me. It's not like it matters anyway."

"He said he heard you slept with half the

UCC rugby team and that your baby could be anyone's. He also said that you purposefully got pregnant by him so you could try to get his money to raise your half-breed baby."

Luna's face turned bright red, but she shrugged and took a deep breath.

"It's fine. I don't need him to accept us." She rubbed her belly.

"I know that, Luna. And he was obviously just panicking and trying to cover his ass. But we did exactly what we wanted to do."

Luna looked at her curiously.

"And what's that?"

Issy smiled.

"We told him exactly what he did. We told him that we knew what he did to you, Luna. We confronted him."

"Well, you did."

Issy put an arm around her shoulder.

"Nope. You're my sister. They were your words, Luna. I just spoke them for you."

Luna nodded as they walked into the house.

Chapter 17

Meeting Dr. Preston

"Luna Begay, come to the office, please. Thank you."

Luna looked up from her Math book, frowning.

"Luna?" her teacher called out from her desk.

Luna shrugged.

"Better go see what they want," her teacher smiled.

Luna smiled back and stood up, grabbing

her notebook and backpack. She walked to the office, not quite sure what she was going to find when she got there. She opened the door and stepped inside with some trepidation . . . which increased when she saw her mother standing at the counter.

"Mom! Is everything okay? Is it Dad?"

Her mother frowned in confusion.

"What? No, honey. Everything's fine. I'm taking you to the doctor."

"Why? I'm fine."

"You need to see an obstetrician, Luna. We have to make sure the baby is okay."

Luna's hands flew to her belly.

"Do you think he's not okay?"

"I'm sure he's fine. But you haven't been to a doctor yet and we need to take care of both of you."

Luna rubbed her stomach.

"Yeah, alright."

***

The doctor's office was nicer than she had expected. It was full of women of various shapes and sizes. Some still had flat stomachs. Some had tiny, round bumps. And many had huge, full stomachs that looked like they couldn't possibly stretch another millimetre. Luna looked at her mom, unsure what she should do. Her mom led her over to the receptionist.

"Hi. Luna Begay to see Dr. Preston, please."

The woman handed her mom a clipboard and a cup.

Luna frowned at the cup. "What's that for?"

The receptionist looked amused.

"Take it into one of the bathrooms over there and urinate in it, then take it to the desk there. Just leave it on the counter."

Luna took it, blushing.

Minutes later, she sat down beside her mom and looked over her shoulder at the forms she was filling out. Luna tried to resist looking at all the other women, but failed. She was definitely the youngest person in the room. The youngest patient anyway. She watched a tiny baby, asleep in a carrier, smiling in its sleep.

"Luna? Can you come with me, please?" The receptionist was standing now. "Mrs. Begay, you can wait here for now."

Luna reluctantly left her mother and walked over.

"Right through there," the nurse said. "Go ahead into room three and you can take everything off and put on the gown. Someone will be in shortly."

Luna stepped hesitantly into the examining room and looked around. It was just like any other doctor's room. She took her clothes off and folded them carefully. She pulled the gown on, tying it around herself tightly. She stood in the middle of the room as the door flew open and a tiny tornado of a woman entered.

"Hi, Luna. I'm Carrie." She was talking

before she was even in the room and Luna barely had time to register a mane of brilliant auburn hair before she was behind her and out of her line of vision.

"Umm. Hi?"

She craned her neck, but Carrie was still moving. Just as Luna gave up trying to catch a glimpse, she popped up beside her and grinned. She was younger than Luna had expected. Her nose was dusted with freckles and she had the greenest eyes she'd ever seen. She was dressed casually in jeans and a sweater that looked so soft, Luna was tempted to reach out and stroke her sleeve.

"So, I'm just going to weigh you and check your blood pressure. Do you have any questions for me?"

"No. Not yet."

Carrie nodded and wrapped a blood pressure cuff around her arm. She inflated it and pulled the stethoscope from around her neck to listen.

"Good! Your blood pressure is normal. Can you step on the scale for me, please?"

Luna stepped onto the scale and watched as Carrie moved the metal weights over.

"So you've gained about twelve pounds so far."

"*Twelve?*" Luna was shocked. "But I don't eat junk food or anything. How is that possible?"

Carrie smiled.

"Twelve is actually really good. It's normal; don't worry. We'd be concerned if you were gaining too much or not enough, but you're doing really well, Luna. Okay. Hop up on the table and I'll be right back."

Hop? Luna climbed onto the stepstool and inched her way backward onto the table. She had just started looking around at all of the posters on the wall depicting women with wedding rings placed firmly on their left hand, rubbing their protruding bellies while their delighted-looking husbands beamed proudly at them, when Carrie came back in.

"Umm . . . will the doctor be in soon?" she asked nervously.

Carrie looked at her in surprise and laughed.

"I'm so sorry! I'm your doctor, Luna."

Luna coloured.

"Oh! I'm sorry. You said your name was Carrie . . . and you're so young! I was expecting . . ."

"An old guy with a beard? Don't worry. It happens all the time. If it makes you feel better, you can call me Dr. Preston. But Carrie is fine, too. Now we need to check on your baby. Your mom is waiting outside but she's going to come after we do a quick pelvic exam. Have you had one of those before?"

Luna shook her head.

"That's okay. I just need to examine your cervix. Sounds awful but it won't hurt and I'll be quick. So, I just need you to lie back and slide all the way down for me. Perfect."

Luna closed her eyes and tried to think of anything other than the fact that a total stranger was looking at her cervix. The doctor stood up and took her rubber gloves off with a sharp snap, tossing them into the trash can.

"You can put your clothes back on, Luna. Everything seems good. If it's okay with you, I'm going to bring your mother in now. We're going to do an ultrasound and I thought you might want her with you for that."

"Wait! I was wondering . . . well, we're, umm . . . Aboriginal? Is it bad to have burning sage or anything around?"

Carrie smiled.

"I don't think that would be a problem."

Luna nodded.

"Okay. And will the hospital let me play traditional music in the delivery room?"

"Well, I'll be the one delivering your baby, so definitely. Whatever makes you most comfortable, okay?"

Luna nodded her thanks while Carrie left

the room. She dressed quickly and was back up on the table when Dr. Preston knocked. She opened the door, ushering her mother, and another young-looking girl in scrubs, into the room with her.

"Lie back down, Luna. Mrs. Begay, you can stand beside her. Up near her head if you don't mind. Luna, this is Cindy, our ultrasound technician extraordinaire. She's going to give us a look at your baby. Cindy, go ahead."

The girl smiled at Luna and squeezed a glob of jelly onto her stomach, making her gasp.

"I know. I'm sorry. It's always cold when we put it on." She laughed at Luna's expression and picked something up off the machine beside the bed.

"So, we're just going to run this transducer over your stomach so we can get a picture of your baby and do some measurements."

Luna looked at her mother. She was torn. She was dying to see her baby but she was also terrified. *What if something is wrong?* Cindy placed the transducer on her stomach and started moving it around, watching the screen intently, only taking her eyes off the screen to murmur something to the doctor or write something down. Luna glanced at her mother nervously. Her mom smiled back and took her hand. Neither Carrie nor Cindy looked concerned, but maybe they just didn't want to scare her.

"Ummmm . . . is everything okay?" Luna asked timidly.

"Sorry, Luna. Yes, the baby looks fine. Cindy was just writing some measurements down in your file." She turned the screen toward them. "That's your baby."

Luna stared at the screen and the breath went out of her. There was her baby. He was lying on his back, waving his hands around. He arched his neck and she could see his profile clearly. His tiny nose and his little lips. As she watched, he raised his hand toward his face.

Carrie smiled at her. "Your baby is sucking its thumb."

Luna's mouth dropped open and she looked over at her mother. Her mom was staring at the screen, tears running down her face.

"Mom?"

She turned to look at Luna and smiled. Cindy hit a button and the room was suddenly filled with a galloping, steady beat.

"That's your baby's heartbeat," she said, smiling. "Do you want to know the sex?"

Luna nodded, watching her baby moving around on the screen.

"You're having a little boy, Luna."

Luna laughed. A deep, genuinely happy sound.

"I knew it," she said.

Chapter 18

The Hardest Decision

Ten minutes later, they were sitting in Dr. Preston's office. Luna was clutching a photo from the ultrasound and staring at it, a smile on her face. Carrie looked at her, then at her mother.

"Luna, I know this is a hard conversation, especially right after your first ultrasound. But what are your plans for the baby?"

Luna was jolted away from the photo and back into reality. She glanced over at her mother, then back at Dr. Preston. She sighed.

"I'm not sure. I kind of tried to hide it until now, so . . . no. I haven't made any definite plans yet." She was embarrassed and wished she had a better answer for her.

"You're not the first young mother we've had in here, Luna. You're not even the first one we've seen today. But you're almost in your third trimester. You're lucky that you and your baby are both healthy but you can't pretend he doesn't exist anymore." She was smiling kindly as she said this. "You need to sit down with your parents and talk. If you want to keep him, we can help you find resources for young mothers, and if you want to consider adoption, we can recommend an agency to help you find the right parents for him. I know this is hard. I know you must feel pulled in a million different directions. I know you're confused. But time is running out." She handed her a pile of pamphlets and brochures. "Take a look at these. Go through them with your family.

And talk. Sit down and start talking about your options."

Luna nodded and took the brochures from her.

"Thanks," she said. "We'll look at them." She glanced at her mother, who nodded back.

"Great. Then I'll see you in a couple of weeks." Carrie shook hands with them and showed them back into the waiting room.

They walked out together. Quiet. Thoughtful. Luna's head was full of the experience of seeing her baby and hearing his heartbeat. It was finally hitting her that, in three short months, he was going to be here. And she had no clue what she was going to do, but she secretly suspected, deep in her heart, that she wasn't ready to be a mother.

"Luna?" Her mother broke into her reverie.

"Yeah?"

Her mother reached into her bag and handed her an envelope.

"This came for you today."

Luna took it, glancing down at the return address and the logo boldly stamped on it. She looked up at her mom.

"It's from McGill University!"

Her mother nodded.

"I know."

Luna tore the envelope open and quickly scanned the letter. She handed it to her mother, her eyes filling with tears.

"I got in!"

✳ ✳ ✳

Luna spent that night reading the brochures that the doctor had given her, googling adoption and teen mothers, reading statistics and message boards, and leafing through the materials that McGill had sent. The more she read, the more she realized that, although she loved this baby already, she didn't really believe that she was ready to raise him. If she was being completely honest with herself, she knew that she had no way to provide the kind of life that she wanted for him. In the back of her mind, she had known it all along.

Sleep didn't come easily that night and Luna went down to the kitchen in the morning with dark circles under her eyes, her hair tangled around her face. Her mother looked up from the stove where she was scrambling eggs.

"Are you okay?"

Luna grunted in response and sat down at the table. Her father eyed her cautiously. He opened his mouth and closed it again. Normally a man of few words, he was even less talkative in the morning.

"Didn't you sleep, honey?" her mother asked.

"Not really." She yawned hugely.

Issy walked into the kitchen, already dressed and ready to go. She did a double take at Luna as she grabbed a box of cereal out of the cupboard.

"Whoa! You look awful."

"Thanks a lot."

"Sorry."

Issy held up the cereal to her, raising her eyebrows. Luna nodded and Issy poured her a bowl.

"You were up looking at those brochures and stuff." It was a comment, not a question.

Luna nodded. Her sister exchanged glances with their mother.

Her mother sat across from her and took her hand. "Have you made any decisions? Or maybe you have some questions?"

"I just . . . I don't feel like I can raise him myself. But if someone else raises him, they'll be sharing their culture with him. He'll never know his own heritage. He won't know where he comes from or our history."

Her eyes filled with tears as her mother came around the table to give her a hug.

"I know, Luna. I've thought of that too. But that's the sacrifice you'd be making. He won't be raised in our culture . . . but if he wants to learn about it someday, he will."

Luna nodded slowly.

"I think I already knew what I was going to do."

Issy looked surprised.

"You do?"

"Yeah. I'm going to call the adoption agency that the doctor recommended."

Her mother nodded as Issy glanced up.

"What? Why?" Issy asked.

"Because I can't give him the life he deserves! I'm seventeen! I want to get an education and be able to provide for a family someday."

"We could help you! I told you that!" Issy's face was bright red. "Right, Mom?"

She stared hard at their mother, who took a drink of her coffee before answering.

"Yes. Of course. If you want to keep the baby, we'll help you. We'd find a way."

"How, Mom? You and Dad are never here

and we're already tight on money."

"I could quit school." Issy and Luna exchanged shocked looks. "Just for now. Until he's older. And Dad could work something out. Maybe just work nights?"

He nodded.

Luna leaned over and hugged her mother.

"No. It's one thing for me to make sacrifices. But I'm not asking you to give up your dreams too. You either, Issy. Mom is going to be a nurse. Dad's shop is going to be a huge success. You're going to be a fashion designer. And . . . I think I want to take Women's Studies and Native Studies. I was thinking maybe I could work with other Aboriginal girls. Rape victims or young mothers . . . I haven't figured it out yet. But this baby deserves a better life than I can give him. I don't have a job and there's no way I could make more than minimum wage. I'm still a kid myself. I don't think that emotionally I'm ready to be a mom."

She looked around the table as she said

this. Her mother and Issy were nodding but her father was looking at the floor.

"Dad?" He looked up at her, his eyes wet. "Dad! What's wrong?" Luna wanted to cry.

He tried to smile.

"I respect your decision. But . . . I can't help but wonder if that baby is going to grow up thinking he wasn't loved? I know you're only seventeen, Luna. I believe that you're making the right decision for yourself and that you're trying to put this baby first. I know you're worried he won't learn about his culture, but I can't stand the idea that he'd think you didn't want him. That *we* didn't want him."

Tears slid down Luna's face as she listened to her father say more to her than he had in months. She pushed her chair back from the table and went to her father. She hugged him hard.

"I'm so sorry, Daddy. I don't want you to be sad. I don't want the baby to think we don't love him but he deserves a better life than I can give him. And better parents than I can be."

Her father wiped his eyes, then brushed at a tear on Luna's face.

"I know. I'm proud of you. I don't know if I could have made that decision. You'll be a great mother someday, Luna. When you're ready."

Chapter 19

Meet the Parents

As the car turned onto St. Germain, Luna stared out the window at the perfectly manicured emerald-green lawns. The houses were truly magnificent with basketball nets in the driveways and chalk drawings on the sidewalks. There was a playground at the end of the street that was full of children climbing, sliding, and swinging.

"Well, this looks nice," her mother called out with forced cheerfulness.

Her father nodded back.

"Okay. This is it."

He pulled their ancient Jeep Patriot behind a brand-new silver BMW in the driveway of a stunning house. There was something comforting about this neighbourhood. The houses may be larger than hers and the cars newer, but Luna couldn't help but smile at a young mother pushing a stroller and singing the ABCs loudly to her baby. Everywhere Luna looked there were children laughing and playing on the sidewalks or in the park down the street. This was the kind of place where she could see her son being happy. It was the kind of place she'd like to raise children in someday.

Her father opened her car door and held out his hand. "Ready?"

Luna took it and let him help her out of the car. They walked up the stone steps to the front door and rang the doorbell. "Ode to Joy" rang out, the sound muffled by the giant wooden door. Luna heard footsteps approaching and her heart sped up, galloping wildly. The baby did a somersault inside her, sensing her nervousness. The door swung open and a smiling couple greeted them.

"Hi!" the woman enthusiastically welcomed them with a hug. "I'm Lane and this is my husband, Ryan."

He stuck his hand out to them, smiling.

"And you must be Luna! Thanks so much for coming. Please . . . come in," said Lane.

She ushered them through the foyer and into the house. It was a large house with high ceilings and hardwood floors. The walls were decorated with photos of Lane and Ryan mugging for the camera, arms wrapped around each other, their faces lit up with huge smiles.

Lane led them into their living room. There was a soft rug on the floor and a comfy, deep sofa with matching chairs. Luna had expected such a big house to be cold and antiseptic, like Jon's had been. She had pictured oil paintings on the walls, Persian rugs on the floor, and cold, white furniture. Lane and Ryan's house was the complete opposite of Jon's. It was warm and inviting. *They* were warm and inviting. There were plates of cookies, vegetables, fruit, crackers, and cheese laid out on the coffee table. Ryan saw Luna eyeing it and smiled.

"We didn't know what you liked so we got a bit of everything. Help yourself. Can I offer you something to drink? We have tea, lemonade, club soda, orange juice, milk?"

"I'd love some milk, please," Luna smiled.

Lane sat across from Luna and took a cookie.

"So, Luna . . . what are you hoping to study at university?"

Luna took the glass of milk from Ryan.

"Thank you. Umm . . . well, I always planned on taking English Literature." She took a sip of her milk.

"Really? That's what my degree is in!"

"But I've kind of been thinking of

changing it to a double major in Women's and Native Studies."

"That's amazing, Luna. I took some Native Studies courses as well."

Luna looked at her, surprised.

"You did?"

"Yeah. We've got some Indigenous blood in our family so I wanted to learn more about it."

Luna glanced at her parents, her eyes wide.

Lane smiled at Luna and they were soon chatting about books they had read and stories they wanted to write. Luna started to relax and nibbled on a homemade chocolate chip cookie. Her parents were talking to Ryan about places they'd travelled and their dream destinations. She liked it here. She could imagine her baby here, with these people who loved to read, loved to travel, and loved to laugh. Lane even had some Aboriginal ancestry! And they obviously loved each other. She watched as Ryan smiled at his wife and kissed her hand. She saw Lane touch Ryan's arm and look up at him lovingly.

It was a good home. A good family.

Her breath hissed out as the baby gave a huge kick, as if agreeing with her. She rubbed at something protruding out of her stomach. A little elbow or a foot probably.

Lane leaned forward, tentatively.

"May I?" she asked.

Luna looked up at her, surprised by the look of longing on Lane's pretty face.

"Yeah, of course."

She took Lane's hand and put it on top of the spot where the baby was poking something out at them. Lane gasped, her face full of wonder. She glanced up at her husband as the baby shifted under her hand, tears filling her eyes. She smiled at Luna.

"That's amazing," she said, laughing through her tears.

Ryan stood behind his wife and kissed the top of her head.

"Do you want to feel him too?" Luna asked him.

"Of course!"

He walked around the couch and crouched beside her. He put his hand on her stomach and was rewarded with a sharp kick. He pulled his hand back and looked at Luna in shock.

She laughed.

"I think he likes you," she told him.

He sat down across from her.

"Thank you, Luna. I've never felt that before. So . . . do you have any questions for us?" He looked at her parents as well. "Any of you?"

Luna sat back, sinking into the couch and stroking the baby-soft blanket draped over the arm.

"Well . . . I guess I wondered why you were adopting?" She looked up quickly. "Is it okay if I ask that?"

Ryan and Lane exchanged glances. He leaned over and kissed his wife's cheek, then smiled at Luna.

"Of course. Right after we got married,

Lane was diagnosed with ovarian cancer. After chemo failed, they had to perform a hysterectomy. It saved her life and she's been cancer-free for five years."

Luna looked at Lane. This beautiful, young woman was so full of life. She never would have guessed that she was a cancer survivor.

"I'm so sorry," she said.

Lane smiled at her.

"I came to terms with it years ago. I'm not able to get pregnant, obviously, but we always knew we wanted to be parents. We've been lucky. Ryan's company is doing well and I get to write for a living, so I'm home all the time. We have a home we love. We just want to be a family."

Luna nodded thoughtfully. All she wanted was for her son to have the best family possible. A family who would love him and treasure him and give him all the things she couldn't. She could see her son growing up in a place like this, with these people. They were full of life and laughter and love. There was nothing more she could possibly want for him. She took a deep breath.

"If I gave you a letter to give to him someday . . . would you do that? When he's older? And maybe tell him about his culture?"

She was afraid to hope that they might agree, that her son might know someday how heartbreaking this decision was for her. That he might know how much she loved him.

Lane took her hand.

"Of course we will. I'm sure when he's older, he'll want to know more about you and where he came from."

A tear slid down Luna's face. She smiled through her tears and squeezed Lane's hand.

"I think you'll be amazing parents," she said.

Chapter 20

We're Having a Baby

It was silent in the house. The moon was shining brightly through the window into the dark bedroom where the girls were fast asleep. Luna was dreaming that she was feeding a horse a lump of sugar . . . a horse that turned and kicked her squarely in the stomach.

She gasped, suddenly wide awake, and clutched her stomach. It was hard as a rock and it hurt so badly that she felt like she couldn't breathe.

"Issy!" she hissed through clenched teeth, her voice barely above a whisper. She was doubled over on the bed, trying not to scream, when the pain started to fade. A minute later, it was gone and she stretched back out on the bed in relief. Maybe she could get back to sleep now. She closed her eyes and breathed deeply.

Just as she was drifting off, her stomach tightened up again and a bolt of pain shot through her. She held her breath, her hands clutching at the sheets. She opened her mouth to call out for Issy, or for her mother, but no sound came out until the pain eased up again.

She rose this time, rolling onto her side so she could sit up and ease herself off the bed. She waddled to Issy's bed and shook her.

"Issy," she called, needing to get the words out before the pain overtook her again. "Is!"

Issy's eyes fluttered open just as a gush of water poured down Luna's legs.

"What's going on? Are you okay?" Issy sat up, taking in her sister's pale, pinched face.

"I'm having contractions. And I think my water just broke."

Issy's mouth dropped open.

"Get Mom!"

Issy sprang from her bed and ran from the room. She was back a moment later with their mother. Luna was bent over, clutching her stomach and moaning. Her mom rushed over and rubbed her back, murmuring soft words to her.

"Hang on, minôs. It'll pass. Just breathe, Luna."

Luna nodded. Issy looked like she was going to pass out.

"They're really close together, Mom," Luna moaned.

She glanced at Issy.

"Grab her bag and call your father. We're going to the hospital as soon as Luna can walk."

Issy picked up her phone and dialled.

"Dad? Luna's having the baby. We're taking her to the hospital. Okay. Okay. Bye." She hung up. "He'll meet us there."

"Good. Okay, Luna. Can you walk now? We need to get you to the hospital."

"I don't want to have my baby in the car!" she cried.

Her mother laughed.

"It'll be a while yet, I think. But let's get going just in case."

She helped Luna down the stairs and into the front seat of the car. Luna reclined it and tried to get comfortable.

"We'll be there in five minutes, honey. I know a shortcut."

She sped off, one hand holding tightly onto Luna's.

***

Luna lay on a hospital bed, her knees pulled up, and cried out in pain as another contraction wracked her body. Sweat plastered her hair to her forehead, and after two hours of labour, she didn't even care anymore that people were walking in and out of the room and staring under her gown. She panted with exhaustion as the contraction eased again. Her mother fed her ice chips and wiped her forehead with a cold cloth.

"You're doing great, Luna." She smiled lovingly at her.

"Why won't they give me an epidural? I can't stand this anymore. Please! I have to push!" she begged.

The nurse looked up from the fetal heart monitor.

"You're too close, Luna. You're almost fully dilated. It's too late for an epidural. I'm so sorry. The doctor is coming back to check you out again in a minute and we should be able to start pushing that baby out soon."

Luna looked at her mother in panic.

"I don't think I can do this, Mom," she cried. "I'm scared."

Her mother wiped her brow again.

"You can, sweetheart. Everything is going to be fine."

Dr. Preston walked in a moment later and looked under her gown.

"You're fully dilated, Luna. Everything is going perfectly. We're going to get ready and you can start pushing."

She turned to speak to the nurse. The room was a hive of activity as they rushed around. Carrie adjusted her stool and smiled at Luna as she patted her leg.

"I know this is scary but I do this all the time. I promise it'll be okay."

Luna grimaced as another contraction hit her.

"Okay, Luna . . . this time I want you to push. Bear down . . . hold your breath if you need to and push as long as you can."

Luna did as she was told. Her body tensed up as she held onto her mother's hand and pushed. She cried out, panting as the contraction ebbed.

"That's great, sweetheart," her mother said. "I'm so proud of you, Luna. You're doing great."

"You are, Luna. That was perfect," Carrie said. "We have another contraction coming, so get ready to push again."

Luna moaned as the next contraction washed over her. Grunting with the effort, she held her breath, clenched her teeth, and pushed. A cry escaped her as she put everything she could into pushing.

"I can't do this," she cried as soon as she could catch her breath again. "Please don't make me do this!" she begged her mother.

"I wish I could help you, sweetie. But you're doing great."

The doctor was doing something under her gown. She could feel her hands moving between her legs.

"Okay, Luna. Next contraction, we're going to try to get the head out, okay? So I want you to push extra hard."

She was exhausted. "I can't," she panted.

Carrie smiled up at her.

"Yes, you can. We're all here to help."

She felt the contraction coming and sobbed out a big breath.

"Okay, Luna. Push hard."

She gritted her teeth, dropped her chin to her chest and pushed.

"Perfect! The head is out, Luna. I'm just going to reach in and help with the shoulders now."

She looked up at her mother again but was so exhausted, she couldn't even think of any words.

"Okay. One more time. One big push and we'll have your baby out, Luna. You can do this."

Her mom was murmuring to her, encouraging her, and Carrie was feeling around and trying to help from the end of the bed. The contraction was completely overwhelming and Luna was so tired. But she took a deep breath and — sitting up as much as she could — dropped her chin again, closed her eyes and cried out with the effort of pushing.

"Keep pushing, Luna!" the doctor called out.

Luna felt the pain thankfully ease up at the same time she heard a cry from the end of the bed. She collapsed back onto the bed as her mother and Carrie called out words of praise that barely registered with her.

"Can I see him?" she whispered.

The nurse took the baby from the doctor and walked to the other side of the room.

"Of course. You can hold him as soon as we get him cleaned up and weighed. You did great, Luna."

Her mother was crying and stroking her head lovingly.

"I'm so proud of you, Luna."

The nurse came back a moment later with a tiny blue-wrapped bundle in her arms. Luna struggled to sit up and see her son. Her mother propped the pillows higher as the nurse handed her the most gorgeous baby she had ever seen. He looked up at her with his sky-blue eyes, his ebony lashes blinking against his cheeks. Luna kissed his head.

"Isn't he beautiful?" she asked no one in particular.

Her mother nodded and reached her hand out, brushing her fingers against the baby's cheek.

"The most beautiful baby in the world," Luna whispered. "I love you, little boy."

She kissed her son's tiny head and held him as if she never wanted to let him go.

Epilogue

It was finally quiet. The hospital halls were dimly lit and sparsely populated. Luna made her way to the nursery, careful not to move too quickly. She was sore; her body ached in places she hadn't even known existed. So much was different now. Not only since yesterday, but also during the past nine months. That one night had changed her forever. Instead of breaking her, it had just made her stronger. She was strong enough to make the most difficult decision of her life for her son. She was strong enough to help other girls like her someday.

There was only one nurse on duty in the nursery. She smiled at Luna from a chair where she was scribbling notes on a clipboard. Luna walked over to the bassinets and immediately saw Baby Boy Begay asleep with a blue knit cap over his perfect head.

She stood over the bassinet, looking down at her sleeping son. His long, coal-black eyelashes lay on his soft cheeks and his tiny rosebud mouth moved as he dreamed.

She reached down and touched his smooth cheek, then pulled her hand back as his eyes opened suddenly. He looked up at her curiously. He was absolutely perfect. He was swaddled in a blue blanket, wrapped tightly, with one hand free. She reached down and touched his tiny hand. He wrapped his fingers around hers and held on, still watching her.

The nurse walked up behind her.

"He needs to be fed," she whispered.

"Oh. Okay." Luna, reluctant to let go, took her hand away from him and gave him one last look.

"Would you like to feed him?" the nurse asked.

Luna looked at her, torn between holding her son one last time and escaping back to her room. She nodded.

"Yes. Thank you."

She sat down in one of the rocking chairs while the nurse picked up the baby. She handed him to Luna and helped her settle him properly in her arms. She held the bottle out to her and smiled.

"Here you go. I'll be over there if you need help."

Luna couldn't take her eyes off her son. She held the bottle to his mouth, touching his lips. He opened his mouth eagerly and started drinking, staring up at her. She felt a painful pressure in her chest as she watched him drink and sighed deeply. She'd have to pump again soon. She watched his lips move against the bottle, stroked his cheek, and kissed his downy head. His fingers wrapped around her thumb and Luna smiled sadly at him as tears flooded her eyes. Tomorrow, he'd be going home with Lane and Ryan. Leaving the hospital and leaving her. She took a deep breath and looked around. The nurse was on the phone, not paying any attention to her.

"Hi, baby," she said, looking into her son's eyes. "I love you so much. I hope you know that. I hope you know how hard it is giving you up. If I was older and could take better care of you . . . if I could give you the life you deserve, I'd keep you. But I can't. I'm only seventeen. Lane and Ryan are going to take good care of you. They love you and they're going to be the best parents in the world. I promise. They're going to teach you about our culture and you're going to be proud of your heritage. Lane even hung the dreamcatcher I made above your crib. And someday, when you're older, they'll tell you all about me and how I loved you with all my heart."

She leaned down and kissed the top of his head, breathing him in, feeling his heartbeat pulsing against her lips.

"I will never forget you. I'll never forget this moment when I got to be your mom. I will love you forever. I know you're going to have an amazing, happy life. I wish . . ."

She didn't even know what she wished. That she was older? That she could support and care for this tiny little guy herself? That she'd see him grow up?

"I just wish things were different."

He had finished his bottle and his eyes were fluttering closed as he yawned.

The nurse walked over, holding her phone in her hand.

"I can take a picture . . . if you want?"

Luna looked up at her.

"More than anything," she said.

She smiled and held her son as the nurse

snapped a picture, then took her e-mail address to send it to her.

"I should get him back to bed," the nurse said, gently. "If you're ready."

Luna nodded. She kissed him once more, breathing the smell of him in, willing herself to remember this moment. She nuzzled her face against him.

"I love you, baby," she whispered as she said goodbye to her son for the last time.